An Outraged Candie

"You're no gentleman!"

"Shall I reply with the obvious?" crooned Tony, still advancing on her, not stopping until he had effectively backed her into a corner of the room. "You asked why I am here tonight. I think we are both about to discover the answer."

Candie pressed herself against the wall, her blonde head slowly moving back and forth in wordless denial of the inevitable. She should scream for help. She should faint away at his feet. She should give him a swift kick in the shins.

So why did she feel more awake, more alive than ever before? Why, if there was any contact to be made between the two of them, did she want it to be with her lips, her arms, her tinglingly anticipating body?

Other Regency Romances from Avon Books by
Kasey Michaels

THE BELLIGERENT MISS BOYNTON
THE LURID LADY LOCKPORT
THE RAMBUNCTIOUS LADY ROYSTON
THE SAVAGE MISS SAXON
THE TENACIOUS MISS TAMERLANE

THE MISCHIEVOUS MISS MURPHY

KASEY MICHAELS

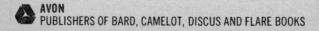 AVON
PUBLISHERS OF BARD, CAMELOT, DISCUS AND FLARE BOOKS

AVON BOOKS
A division of
The Hearst Corporation
1790 Broadway
New York, New York 10019

To Anna Elizabeth Seidick—one
feisty Irish lady—with love.

Prologue

"PAST ONE O'CLOCK and almost two; my masters all good day to you." The feeble voice of the ancient Charlie of the Watch carried no more than a few yards through the dark night and swirling mist that had settled over the city. Looking about himself hesitantly, wondering if he really wanted to see anything besides the yellowish mist hanging about the dim gaslight on the corner, the Charlie wished for the hundredth time that he had been able to resist the bribe that had convinced him to leave his sentry box.

Somewhere close by, a crime was being committed; he knew it as surely as he knew his own name. But he had been paid to call out the time at regular intervals in order to block out any inadvertent noise the burglar (or murderer; he didn't wish to know which) might make, and gold was gold, no matter whose pocket had held it last. He wasn't proud of what he was doing, but then a proud man would never have bribed his way into the Watch in the first place.

He cleared his throat to cry out the hour a last time before turning back down Mount Street to return to his sentry box. He had been avoiding his assigned corner diligently for the past quarter hour, long enough for an experienced ken-cracker and his mates to clear a house down to its bare walls, and it was time he remembered that his duty was to protect the inhabitants of Park Street. Besides, if anyone were to raise a hue and cry any time soon, he didn't want it said that Jack Watkins had not been at his post.

Perhaps it was a sudden, belated attack of conscience, perhaps it was not, but when Watchman Watkins caught sight of a human form sliding down the drainpipe of one of the town houses that lined Mount Street near Park, he summoned up all his small store of courage and sidled up behind the housebreaker just as the man's stocking-clad feet hit the flagway. Clapping a shaking hand on the thief's shoulder, the stalwart member of the Watch pronounced in the best tradition of his comrades, "Halt, you thievin' rascal. Yer under arrest!"

Tony Betancourt, who had just then been bending over to retrieve his Hessians (and offering up a solemn entreaty that they had not suffered any scuffs due to being tossed from dear Bessie's boudoir window, else his valet Lovell would be inconsolable), remained in his crouched position, merely swiveling his dark head about slightly to get a clear look at his captor. Eyes as dark as the moonless night raked up and down the small, grey-haired watchman whose stern expression did little to overshadow the fact that his knobby knees were shaking like dry bones in a sack. Giving his handsome head a sharp shake, the captive smothered a grin and sighed mournfully. "You got me, Charlie, right and tight. Is it the guardhouse for me, or d'you think I'll swing?"

Jack Watkins was already having second thoughts about both his impromptu action and his well-dressed prisoner. He hadn't put the arm on a ken-breaker, thank the Lord, else it was Lombard Street to a china orange that Mother

Watkins would already be a widow. What he had stumbled on, he was instantly sure, was a nobleman out on a spree, probably cuckolding his best friend, if the truth be told. At least, Jack thought with relief, I didn't nabble him *before* his toss in the hay and ruin his lordship's fun. It wouldn't do to make such a strapping specimen angry. Besides, it was a young buck he had caught, with the light of the devil peeking from his eyes, and if Watkins was very, very lucky, the gentleman would laugh the whole incident off as a part of the thrill of evening.

Just as Mr. Watkins was about to open his mouth to shoo the gentleman on his way, there came a loud commotion from around the corner on Park Street, and from the hysterical female screams and irate masculine bellows that reached the watchman's ears, he knew that a burglary had been discovered—and with him not in his sentry box on the corner! There was nothing else for it; he would have to use the romancing gentleman as his excuse, his reason for deserting his assigned post. So instead of the apology and offer to vacate that he had been about to voice, Jack Watkins opened his mouth to quaver bravely, "Don't ya go doin' anythin' dumb, mister. Yer my prisoner, right 'n' tight. Now, march ta the corner."

Tony Betancourt had a lot of choices open to him at that moment. He could lope off easy as you please, with no fear that the ancient Charlie could catch him. He could stay and explain why he was caught in the act of descending Lady Bledsoe's drainpipe—an embarrassing but plausible explanation. He could...

Suddenly, from the window directly above their heads came the voice of Lord Bledsoe, a man whose biceps were the envy of all London (biceps acquired, so it was said, from the number of whippings he was forced to deliver to gentlemen who had caught his wife's favor). Clearly, Lord Bledsoe was upset about something, and when Tony Betancourt suddenly remembered the greatcoat he had worn earlier in the evening but was not wearing now, his choices became fairly limited.

"Come on, Charlie," the Seventh Marquess of Coniston urged as he scooped up his Hessians and made for the corner, "do your duty, man. Haul me off to the guardhouse!"

Chapter One

SOME FOUR HOURS later, just as dawn was breaking over the city, Tony Betancourt was about to take his leave of the local guardhouse and its bemused head constable. That man was still a trifle dazed after being half bullied and half cajoled into seeing the error of his subordinate's actions in mistaking a Marquess for a common housebreaker. And not just any Marquess, oh no, but the beloved scion of one of the most powerful families in the land (not to mention the grandson of two Dukes and the godson of no less than three of the royal Princes). Jack Watkins had let a band of housebreakers all but denude Sir George Forwood's house in order to collar a titled Lothario, and his superior knew his only pleasure to be had out of this entire episode would be from verbally ripping a strip off the watchman's ignorant hide.

The newly released and still, amazingly, amused Marquess paused at the threshold to the street, his interest mildly piqued at the sight of a middle-aged, foreign-looking gentleman dressed in turban and flowing robes, and the man's strikingly beautiful and obviously irate female companion. Who had the Charlies nabbed now? he thought idly, leaning against the doorjamb and assuming the part of interested bystander. Really, this place was better than having a front seat at Covent Garden for the farce.

"You cannot incarcerate the person of the Maharajah of Budge-Budge," the female was explaining with some heat. "The King shall have your jobs for this insult. Indeed, you will be fortunate if you escape that easily. Such an affront! Such an inexcusable indignity! I blush to call you my countrymen. Why, we English have . . ."

Lord, Tony thought in admiration, what a rare beauty! Waist-length hair more white than blonde swirled around her body like sea foam, its style as unorthodox as the exotic slant of the enormous sherry-colored eyes that dominated her heart-shaped face. In a temper, as the female obviously was at that moment, she was glorious. How would she look in bed heated by another sort of passion? Tony questioned silently, immediately committing himself to answering his own question. And although the sun was up and his belly told him to go somewhere and seek out his breakfast, wild horses could not move him from the spot.

Reluctantly, Tony turned his attention to the girl's companion, whose determined tugging on the sleeve of her cloak had interrupted her fine, impassioned speech. The dark-skinned man spoke a few singsong phrases in some unknown tongue and then lapsed once more into meditative silence. The girl nodded agreement to whatever the man said and, pressing her palms together as if in homage, favored him with a polite bow before turning back to the assistant constable (who was looking rather shaken, with all this talk of Kings and dire punishments and such).

"The Maharajah graciously agrees not to mention this little misunderstanding when he visits Carlton House this evening. But he is fatigued—from his long journey, you

6

know—and wishes a speedy resolution to this, er, unfortunate incident."

"B-but," stammered the assistant constable, "there is still the matter of the price of your food and lodging at The Swan With Two Necks this last sennight. It must be paid."

"The Maharajah has no English money, as I've told you repeatedly. He will settle the bills once he meets with his bankers later today. The innkeeper was precipitate in summoning you," explained the female with the resigned monotone parents used on children who persisted in asking the same question time and again. "Anyone would think the man believed we were not intending to pay. Three pounds six," she sneered, giving her glorious head a toss. "Surely a trifling amount when weighed against the consequences of insulting one of his royal majesty's guests, don't you agree?"

Get out of that one, my good man, Tony prodded silently, looking at the assistant constable in some amusement. There was definitely something havey-cavey going on here, he knew, having already noticed that the Maharajah's dark face looked so very out of place when measured against the lily-white hands clasped so reverently across his ample belly, and if Indians had twinkling green eyes, it was the first the Marquess had heard of it. If that man was the Maharajah of Budge-Budge (if such a benighted Indian village even boasted a Maharajah), then Mark Antony Betancourt was the King of Persia. But the girl—that magnificent creature—what had she to do with his counterfeit highness?

While the assistant constable looked to one of his underlings, who was just then busily inspecting the scuffed toe of his left shoe, Tony pushed himself away from the doorjamb and sauntered leisurely over to the counter. "Here you go, folks," he said cheerily, tossing some coins down on the scarred wood. "Never let it be said we English don't know how to treat visitors to our shores." Turning to bow elegantly toward the pair of imposters, he winked broadly, adding, "If I may offer my services, ma'am, your highness? I would deem it an honor to accompany you back to The Swan to redeem your luggage, which I am sure the Doubting-Thomas innkeeper has confiscated."

The girl looked dubiously at the arm Tony extended to her and then, at a discreet shove from her companion, sweetly smiled her acceptance of his kind offer and placed her hand on his sleeve.

The Maharajah preceded them through the door into the street, and it was not until they were a full block away from the guardhouse that his highness ducked into a narrow alleyway and confronted their rescuer. "And who might you be, laddie?" he asked, a bit of a brogue marking him as Irish.

"Allow me to introduce myself," Tony drawled, bowing once again. "I am Mark Antony."

An irreverent sniff came from the female still holding his arm. "Certainly you are," she said, disbelief evident in her tone. "And *I* am Cleopatra."

Tony smiled, an action that sent sparks of mischief dancing in his dark eyes. "No, you're not," he contradicted, adding, "Cleopatra's m'sister."

The Manchester Defiance was just pulling into the yard as the hackney Lord Coniston had hired arrived at The Swan With Two Necks, and the hustle and bustle of the arriving passengers, mixed with the well-orchestrated pandemonium that marked the inn as the main competition of The Bull and Mouth in Aldersgate in the race to be the finest coaching hostelry in London, caused the Marquess to remember that his bout of drinking and wenching had left him with a fearsome hangover. "I suggest we adjourn to the breakfast room and to some good eggs and ham before speaking with the innkeeper," he said, already making his way toward the front door of The Swan.

"I wouldn't be sorry to get a glass of spirits," the bogus Maharajah seconded happily. "'Tisn't day yet if I haven't had a bit of good Irish whiskey, y'know. None for the gel, y'know, though I'll wager she wouldn't say no to a fine cup of tay."

From the moment the handsome young lord had smiled at her in the alleyway the girl had not spoken a word, remaining mute throughout the journey to The Swan, her thoughts her own. Part of her was thankful for the man's timely intervention, yet another part of her deeply resented his notion that they had indeed been in need of rescue. She thought she had been handling the matter quite well, actually, and would have had them out of their scrape in another few minutes. As she preceded the Marquess into the crowded breakfast room a smile hovered on her full, dusky-pink lips as she recalled the nervous perspiration on the brow of the assistant constable. The intricate ins and outs of bilking her fellow man were just business; it was the fancy footwork of the thing that gave her such a thrill and got her heart to beating in such a delightful way.

After their order was taken by a sleepy barmaid, Lord Coniston formally introduced himself to his guests and then sat back to see if they were going to return the favor. His sally with the girl in the alleyway had caused the Maharajah to break into delighted laughter and, as the girl could have told him, if you make an Irishman laugh, he's yours. And so, instead of running yet another rig on their savior, the Maharajah leaned over confidentially and whispered, "The name is Murphy, my lord. Maximilien P. Murphy, of the County Donegal Murphys, and this lady here is my young niece and ward, Candice Murphy. We thank you for your service. After all, far better a hasty retreat, y'know, than a bad stand."

Miss Candice Murphy, who had been studiously ignoring the Marquess's intent stare, lifted her head to take umbrage with her uncle's statement. "I take exception to that last remark," she cut in defiantly, glowering at Mr. Murphy. "We were coming about nicely before his lordship poked his fine, aristocratic nose where it had no business to be poking." Turning back to the smiling Marquess, she rested her elbows on the table and narrowed her slanted cat-amber eyes. "Let's talk with the buttons off, my lord," she said bluntly. "What's your lay?" At the man's questioning look she expanded angrily, "Your enterprise, your pursuit, your *angle?*"

Tony Betancourt assumed a crestfallen expression. "How you malign me, Miss Murphy. I acted out of good Christian charity only."

Miss Murphy tossed her head and sniffed unbelievingly, "Of course you did. And when the sky falls, we'll all catch larks."

"Here now," her uncle remonstrated, "it's a fine broth of a boy you see before you, Candie. Don't be measuring his lordship's corn by our own bushel, girlie. He wants nothing more of us than to give us a good turn, or me name's not Maximilien P. Murphy."

"Ac-tu-ally," Tony interrupted, leaning forward on his chair, "Miss Murphy is not altogether incorrect. I ask no payment for services rendered, Mr. Murphy, but I had hoped you would satisfy my curiosity. Call me one of life's observers. My interest has been piqued, and I sense a fine story in the tale of your exploits."

Maximilien P. Murphy measured his breakfast companion with the acquired wisdom of a man who need understand the motivations of his fellow creatures and decided the young lord was in earnest. Besides, if there was one thing Max Murphy craved more than his Irish whiskey, it was flattery, and as his niece moaned her defeat, he spread his hands magnanimously, immodestly acknowledging the fact that, indeed, the story of his life was worthy of great interest.

Candie, knowing the only time her uncle told the truth was when he was somehow unable to summon up a lie, kept her head bowed low over her plate as Max began his tale by claiming kinship to every great Murphy that ever roamed the earth. From the barony of Banagh to Marie

Louise O'Murphy (mistress of Louis XV and sometime artist's model), Max was related to them all. Even Candie did not know how much of this was true, seeing as how Murphy was the most common name in Ireland and Max could just as easily have been the second son of a family of itinerant potato farmers.

Tony listened with what looked like rapt attention to Max's tale of sheltered youth passed in luxury suddenly stripped away by, begging his lordship's pardon, some low, conniving Bug (the Irish's none too flattering term for an Englishman). Left without resources, and with little Candie no more than a babe, he had been forced to live by his wits, and had been doing nicely, thank you, for nearly two decades. "You catch us a bit down at the heels at the moment, y'know, but we'll soon right ourselves. But for now, y'know, I think it would be best if the Maharajah of Budge-Budge takes himself on a little holiday." Rising from the table, Max wrapped his robes about himself and said, "If you meant it about our luggage . . ."

Also rising, and after helping Candice out of her chair —earning for himself no more than a curt thank you— Tony pressed, "But what will you both do now?"

"He'll be an inspector of public buildings for a time," Candie supplied, getting a little of her own back from her uncle, who knew that she meant he would roam the streets with nothing to do.

But Maximilien P. Murphy merely laughed, nudging Lord Coniston with his elbow, saying conspiratorially, "A woman's tongue is a thing that does not rust, m'boyo, and don't you go forgetting it either. To listen to her, you'd think I'll next be landing in the spring-ankle warehouse you call Newgate. Not so, y'know, as I've other fish to fry. There's a lot of wisdom inside this head," he ended, tapping his massive turban with his finger.

"That there is, *Uncail,*" his niece piped up, grinning, "and a multitude of sense outside it as well." Looking not in the least penitent, she asked, "And what rig will you be running now, *Uncail?* This pinching of pennies is such a dreadful bore, don't you know."

Instead of answering, Max took up one of the portmanteaus the innkeeper had grudgingly dumped on the floor, winked broadly at Lord Coniston, and repaired to the small room off to one side of the inn, leaving his niece alone with their rescuer.

They stood in silence for a few minutes, Candie idly inspecting the people wandering in and out of The Swan and Tony idly eyeing her. When the tension between them grew annoying, Candie offered nastily, "You're dreadfully in the way, my lord. If you've had enough sport, you may be on about your travels now, and it's not my eyes that will be crying as you fade from sight."

"Why are you such a prickly pear, sweetness?" the Marquess asked in his smoothest, most seductive voice. "Such a ravishing creature as yourself cannot be unaccustomed to admiration. Why have you taken this particular admirer in such dislike?"

Candie stepped back a pace and reexamined the man standing beside her. "It would seem Max has put the fox to mind the geese. If it's a quick tumble in the hay you're after, my fine upstanding lord, might I suggest that redheaded creature standing near the door? She seems eager enough. As for me, there isn't gold enough in all England to even tempt me into doing what you are thinking."

As seductions went, this one wasn't going so well, a deduction Tony attributed to the fact that he had been up all night and was not appearing at his urbane best. He was sure Max and his "niece" had been down on their luck before, with the comely wench commissioned to replenish their pockets by means of assuming the customary horizontal position, but perhaps he had misread their situation. He had seen himself as the closest, most accessible target for her attentions, but if he didn't soon take his foot out of his mouth she would disappear into the bowels of London and he would never know how her white-blonde hair looked when spread out across his pillow. "Please excuse me for my forwardness," he begged prettily, bowing. "You will find that I am nearly always stupid at this hour of the morning. My words were spoken in all admiration, mixed perhaps with a bit of concern for you and your uncle now that you are out on the street with nowhere to go. Can you find it in your heart to forgive me?"

At that moment Max reappeared, dressed to the teeth in the trappings of an Italian nobleman, the only recognizable feature to give him away being those same sparkling green eyes. Executing an elegant leg for his awestruck audience of one (Candie had seen it all before), Max announced in heavily accented English, "I am the Conte di Casals, lately arrived from Florence. You see with you my niece Gina. Would you be so kind as to have some one of these *servitú* load our *bagagli* into a conveyance so we may repair to our *alloggio* that is on your Half Moon Street?" Taking Tony's arm, as the young lord was standing as still as a wax statue, Max made a shooing motion with his free hand that sent his grinning niece scurrying ahead of them into the sunlight before asking his lordship urbanely, "I am considering either Bigelow or Crimpson to set up my cellars. Who, dear sir, do you recommend for my favor?"

"I am all admiration," Tony said honestly as the trio settled back in yet another hired vehicle and headed off toward Half Moon Street. From the top of his head to the tip of his toes, Maximilien P. Murphy was every inch the Italian Count, and it would take a more discerning eye than Lord Coniston's to find any flaw in the appearance the man projected. "But I also confess to being abominably slow. According to your niece, you were without resources. How did you ever command a set of rooms on Half Moon Street?"

The fat is nicely in the fire now, Candie thought, mentally flogging her uncle for giving in to the urge to show himself off in front of this new, unknown outsider. In all her twenty years she could not remember Max exposing

13

himself so—giving away secrets to a total stranger. Their survival depended on snap judgments of people, though, and so far Max's intuition had been dead center on target. Perhaps, she opined, if the man were not so terribly handsome, with the devil's own black eyes dancing in his head, she would trust him more.

While Candie sat in her corner of the crowded hackney and muttered to herself, Max took command of the conversation, magnanimously explaining his method of convincing his prospective landlord that he was not only expected to arrive on this date, but had already paid his first quarter's rent to the man's agent in the City.

"Are we going to stay at number sixty-three again then, *Uncail*?" Candie asked idly. "There's such a pretty view from the front windows there, don't you think?"

Tony's original mission—bedding one Miss Candice Murphy before the week was out—took a backseat to his interest in Uncle Max and this latest scheme. "You've stayed here before? And *paid* for the privilege?" he asked, suddenly in awe of this great trickster.

"Don't be a goose, sir," Candie answered as her uncle went off in a paroxysm of laughter. "We never *pay* for anything. That's the beauty of the thing. Oh, we never bilk honest people—just the money-hungry ones or those who have more gold than they'll ever need."

"Of course," Tony affirmed, trying very hard to look solemn. "But won't the landlord recognize you?"

Max Murphy slapped a beefy hand on his thigh in delight. "O'course not, boyo. Does my darlin' girl here look anything like an African crown prince?"

Tony looked again at the fair skin and fairer hair of Candice Murphy. "Not at all," he answered, confusion in his face.

Max laughed again. "Well, she did last summer!" he fairly shouted and, thoroughly enjoying the dumbfounded expression on the Marquess's face, uncle and niece indulged themselves in their best laugh since before the assistant constable hauled them away to the guardhouse.

Chapter Two

HAVING THE FAMOUS Marquess of Coniston in their train added consequence to Max's impressive impersonation of an Italian Count aghast at the landlord's ignorance of his identity. Indeed, Max's enactment of an Italian tantrum—complete with loud exclamations, florid gestures, and much dramatic wringing of the hands—was truly inspired, earning him and his niece not only a free quarter year's residence at number sixty-three, but the promise of twice-weekly domestic help at no extra charge. It was all Coniston could do to withhold his applause as the landlord, still quaking with fear that the Conte di Casals might still take exception to his shoddy treatment and take his business elsewhere, bowed himself from the cozy first floor apartments.

No sooner had the door closed behind the landlord than did Max turn to Tony with not a trace of humor apparent on his face to, after murmuring only the briefest thanks for all the Marquess had done them, summarily dismiss the man.

Tony, who had been in the process of lowering himself into a comfortable-looking chair, was more than a little taken aback. "Oh," he said, sudden comprehension bringing a slight sneer to his handsome face, "may I take this to mean my services are no longer required? And just when I was beginning to believe you were a cut above the common crook, too. Pity. Well," he ended, sauntering toward the door, "at least you were amusing for a time, until you showed me your true colors."

Candie, who had been in the process of deciding just where to display her one beloved piece of porcelain sculpture, a very pretty rendition of a young girl and her pet kitten reclining on a grassy knoll, hastened to intervene before her uncle made himself a dangerous enemy. "Please, your lordship," she pleaded prettily, taking Tony's arm, "let me explain. The Irish, especially the older, crustier males," she added, directing a nasty look in her uncle's direction, "tend to moodiness, treating people they meet as the greatest of good fellows, only to condemn them as bloody nuisances an hour later. It's a quirk of the species, I believe, one which Uncle Max has elevated to an art form. I should know, as even I am not immune from such treatment. Though personally I believe Max only suffers so because he considers himself a 'bachelor boy'—vowing that, at close to fifty, he is still too young to marry. Please, consider Max as you would a crotchety old maid, and perhaps you can forgive his rudeness."

"Arrah now," Max muttered, giving voice to a decidedly vulgar Irish expression that, perhaps thankfully, had no real meaning. Ripping off his elaborate fake mustache, he stomped into his bedchamber, rudely slamming the door behind him.

Max's departure left Candie and Tony alone in the room, a circumstance that would have had the Irishman pelting hotfoot back to join them if he hadn't already been involved with the planning of his first escapade meant to put the jingle of gold coins back in his pockets.

"A strange man," Tony mused, looking at the closed door, "but, believe it or nay, I think I actually like him. Perhaps there is some flaw in my character heretofore undisclosed that draws me to him."

In her twenty years, Candie Murphy had been, due to her peculiar lifestyle, thrown into company with many, many men—some gentlemen, many more not—and she had no trouble recognizing the difference. The Marquess of Coniston was a gentleman, and would be one even if stripped of his title. That he was also quite the handsomest man she had ever met did not weigh with her, she told herself emphatically, and had nothing to do with her uncharacteristic objection to Max's customary shabby treatment of people whom he had deemed to have served out their usefulness to him. She couldn't explain her actions; she only knew that now that Max had left them alone, she hadn't the faintest notion of what to say to the man.

When the silence became noticeable, Tony tried once more to gain a toehold in the door, so to speak, as a step toward ingratiating himself with Candie. After all, it was plaguey difficult to bed a chit when they weren't even on speaking terms. Max's none too subtle message of "hands off" Tony could accept as only a minor stumbling block in his pursuit of the niece. He would just have to deal directly with her, a distasteful circumstance, what with plain talk of payment for services rendered and such, but it certainly wouldn't set a precedent in Coniston's dealings with females of her ilk. Besides, why would Murphy have left them alone together if he hadn't been engineering an alliance between the two of them?

If Candie, who had been busy calling herself every kind of fool while at the same time racking her brain for something sensible to say to end the silence, had been privy to Tony's thought processes, she would have found her tongue with a vengeance. Because, contrary to what the Marquess believed, although she was of an age when most of her contemporaries were married, she herself could not boast of ever having so much as a single beau. Her uncle had protected her fiercely from the time she had turned fourteen, and when her appearance, formerly thin and rather gawky, had turned soft and curvy, Max had no longer been able to dress her in pants and have anyone believe she was his nephew.

Fortunately for both Tony's aspirations and Candie's romantic dreams, the Marquess, taking note of Candie's show of shyness (surely a sign that she had at some time trodden the boards), decided to play along, taking the slow approach. To this end he suggested a return visit the next day, when hopefully her uncle would be more himself.

"Uncle Max is always himself," Candie quipped, her happiness at the thought of seeing the Earl again freeing her frozen tongue. "That's what's so distressing."

Tony smiled his understanding and then, sobering slightly, asked, "You won't go taking French leave or anything, will you? I mean, I'd hate to come back here tomorrow to find your uncle had decided to do a flit?" The unaccustomed stab of unease—for the Marquess of Coniston was never uneasy—surprised Tony as much as it delighted Candie, who saw this as a sign of his interest in her.

"Good Lord, no. We may have been in a bit of a pucker when first you saw us this morning, but Max has righted us, as usual, and we are settled now at least until winter. And as Max says, 'Never dread the winter until the snow is on the blanket'—which means I should not worry my head unless there is no roof above it. I refuse to concern myself about what we shall do then until the time comes." She shrugged, looking for a moment to be no more than a child, and then smiled, saying philosophically, "With Max, one must learn to simply relax and follow his lead. He's not steered us wrong yet."

"He plays the cards as they are dealt, does he?" Tony opined, feeling a grudging respect for the gamester, and then, bowing from the waist, he took his leave of Miss

Candice Murphy, promising to return before noon the next day.

As he walked to the corner, hoping to flag down a passing hackney, Tony smiled knowingly. Let's see how cold old Maximilien is when I arrive at his door bearing gifts, he thought evilly, visions of Max delivering his niece to him on a platter lending a certain spring to his lordship's steps as he genially tipped his hat to passersby.

Maximilien P. Murphy sat in a corner of the front room, sipping from his third cup of tea as he scowled at his niece. Lord above us, he groaned inwardly, it's a case of April and May with the girl, and I haven't a notion in hell of how to warn her away from the man without breaking her poor, little heart. Ah, Brigette, my dearest sister, how cruel that you died, leaving this ramshackle uncle as the only protector to stand between your Candice and this bad, terrible world!

Unable to sit still as she waited for Lord Coniston's arrival, Candie, oblivious to her uncle's concern, wandered about the room, flicking an imaginary bit of dust from a table and straightening an already-centered lace doily. She had been up with the dawn, poring over her extensive wardrobe—which boasted of costumes that ranged from the sublime to the ridiculous—in search of just the proper ensemble in which to entertain a Marquess.

Crossing to peer at her reflection in the glass over the sideboard, she tilted her head this way and that, wondering if piling her hair atop her head would be more becoming than the style she had adopted—the long, white-gold tresses pulled back simply from her face and tumbling down her back in loose curls. Shaking her head, she decided it was best not to overdo things; besides, her pink muslin morning gown seemed to call for this more casual style. She pressed a hand to her midsection as the butterflies that had taken up residence there fluttered once more, reminding her of her nervousness.

Unbelievable, Max told himself, simply unbelievable. Could this near-hysterical female possibly be the same Candice Murphy who coolly stared down Bow Street Runners and traded quips with her fellow cardplayers while calmly stripping them of their blunt? Where were the nerves of steel that had served to rescue them from endless scrapes when his derring-do had somehow outstripped his usual good luck? A bleeding pity it was to see such a good gamester lose her nerve over a mere man—a real bleeding pity.

"Candie, m'love," Max spoke up at last when he could no longer endure her case of the fidgets, "come sit down here by me a moment. I've got a story I'd like you to hear."

Candie liked her uncle's stories, which was a good thing, considering how very fond he was of telling them, and she grabbed at his offer thankfully. Perhaps, she hoped, Max's fairy tale would be diverting enough to take her mind from the Marquess's visit. Flopping down on the floor beside his chair, she looked up and encouraged sweetly, "Ah, *Uncail*, is it a fantasy you're to weave for me this morning, or yet another legend about the great Maximilien?"

Max didn't return her bantering but merely reached out a hand to pat her fondly on the top of her fair head. How he loved this child of his heart, and if he had done badly by her, it was not that he hadn't given his best. Times were hard, especially for homeless Irishmen, but what God had not given him in material things, He had supplied in an abundance of ingenuity. A quick mind, adept footwork, and a never-ending supply of greedy souls begging to be relieved of their gold had served to keep a roof over their heads and food on the table. Candice had grown into a warm, generous, intelligent person, because or in spite of her uncle's tutelage, but nothing in her life had prepared the girl for Mark Antony Betancourt.

"Once upon a time," Max now began in the age-old

way, "there lived a fine, brawny Irishwoman named Elizabeth Fitzgerald."

"And why would I be thinking you'd tell a story about a fine, brawny *Englishwoman*?" Candie quipped, giving her uncle's knee a small push.

"Don't be interrupting, lass," Max scolded without heat. "Now, where was I? Oh yes. Elizabeth Fitzgerald." He sat back in his chair, warming to the tale he was about to tell. "Well, it seems this Mrs. Fitzgerald lived in a fine castle, in County Cork perhaps, and she was mighty proud of her possession. Then one fine day her husband, who had been out and about somewhere doing the Lord only knows what, ups and gets himself captured by some horse-stealing neighbors, who then surround Elizabeth's castle to tell her she must surrender her fine pile o'stones or else they'll slit her husband's scrawny throat."

"Oh, my," Candie interrupted, "so it's to be a bloody tale then, is it?"

"Ah, colleen, how sadly you mistake the matter," her uncle corrected. "Elizabeth Fitzgerald was as shrewd as she could hold together, so she was, and did not allow her romantic heart to rule her practical head. 'Mark these words,' she called down to the rabble from high atop her splendid castle, 'they may serve your own wives on some occasion. I'll keep my castle. For Elizabeth Fitzgerald may get another husband, *but Elizabeth Fitzgerald may never get another castle!*'" His story done, Max peered down to see Candie's reaction.

Candice Murphy was not slow in taking her uncle's meaning. "I should send him packing? Is that what you're saying, *Uncail?* But I have no castle to lose."

Max stared into her eyes, his own full of unspoken warning. "Don't you, lass?"

London was becoming a bit thin of company, what with gentlemen going off hunting in the wilds whilst their ladies retired to country estates to make a great show of affection over the children they had birthed through duty and then promptly deserted to the care of strangers.

The Marquess of Coniston, his liaison with Lady Bledsoe having prompted him to turn down several invitations to transfer his drinking and wenching to the north of England for a space, found himself to be rather pleased by the lack of hustle and bustle along the usually crowded streets of Mayfair as he tooled his curricle down Half Moon Street. Not having to dodge cow-handed drivers and wave to endless acquaintances left him more latitude for daydreaming for one thing, and for another, it made that many fewer dandies try to cut him out in his pursuit of Candice Murphy, who was bound to cause a stir in his circle of beauty-hungry bucks.

The weather had proved to be unseasonably warm this morning, and he felt certain he could convince Miss Murphy to accompany him on a drive through the Park, away from the watchful eyes of her protector. Once Max Murphy clapped his greedy Irish eyes on the hamper full of fine wine and assorted delicacies from the Coniston kitchens, he would be more prone to see his "niece's" suitor in a favorable light.

After all, Mark Antony Betancourt, Seventh Marquess of Coniston, was flagrantly handsome, obscenely wealthy, and wickedly intelligent. He was also young, healthy, and popular. Friendship with him would render Max an entrée into society he could not dare to cast aside lightly.

What would *not* please Max was the fact that the Marquess was, like his circle of cronies, dedicated to the belief that it was his solemn duty as an English peer to bed as many women as he could during his sojourn upon this Earth.

And to wed none of them.

Lord Coniston—or Tony, as he was affectionately called by his friends—had, since attaining his majority eight years earlier, shown such diligence and dedication to what he saw as quite the most pleasant of the obligations attached to his rank that he had gained himself a second, slightly less endearing nickname.

Within two years of his advent into London society, he was known throughout the *ton* as Mister Overnite, an appellation that was as descriptive of his nocturnal pursuits as it was self-explanatory. Tony Betancourt not only held the distinction of bedding more lightskirts than many other young bucks had eaten hot dinners, but he was also said to hold the modern-day British record for dallying the whole night long in more society matrons' beds than half the husbands in the Upper Ten Thousand.

But today, in this pleasant fall season, Tony had a different sort of game in his sights. I wonder what their true relationship to be, Tony mused as he eased his horses toward the kerb, knowing he disliked the idea that the Murphys could be "kissing cousins." In point of fact, he'd rather Max was no relation at all to the blonde beauty— that would make it easier for him to sever the connection between them. After all, there was something inherently distasteful in having the famous Mister Overnite brought to doing business with a common pimp.

Not that Max Murphy could honestly be called "common." After hopping from his curricle, tossing the reins to a waiting urchin who doffed his cap, promising to guard his lordship's bloods with his life, the Marquess gathered up his basket of bribes and loped up the steps two at a time, surprising himself with his own eagerness to see Candie Murphy again.

The chit makes Bessie Bledsoe take a backseat, and that's a fact, thought Mister Overnite, thereby consigning yet another mistress to the refuse heap without a flicker of regret. Ah well, he acknowledged silently, the thrill lay mostly in the chase anyhow, and with titled ladies nearly falling over themselves to be bedded, dealing with an honest whore was almost refreshing.

The door to the Murphys' rooms opened before he could knock, and Tony was left standing, one fist raised in the air, to stare into the solemn little face of Candice Murphy. Uh-oh, he winced inwardly. From the look on the girl's face, I'd say Max's mood hasn't improved to the point where I'll be welcomed like a long-lost son.

But this was only a passing thought, driven from his mind as he took in the sight of his quarry—looking good enough to eat in a pretty pink confection that would bring tears of envy to any debutante's eyes. If he didn't know better, he'd think the girl to be as innocent as his sister had been before her first Season.

"Lord Coniston," Candie was saying in her low, pleasantly husky voice. "I thought I heard your Hessians on the stair. Here, let me take this from you, if it is indeed for me." Reaching out her hands, she divested him of his basket and walked over to show it to her uncle. "Look, Uncle Max, gifts—and to think he doesn't look the least bit Greek."

Max flashed his niece a quick wink, acknowledging her admission that she agreed with his reading of the man and would thus be on her guard. Reassured, he turned his attention to the contents of the hamper, finding himself to be well pleased by what he saw. No slowtop, the Marquess, Max concluded, eyeing the label of his favorite Irish whiskey, but it would take more than a few drops of Ireland's best to pull the wool over Maximilien P. Murphy's green eyes.

"Elizabeth Fitzgerald would be proud of you, lass, that she would," Max said under his breath. The Marquess might be a handsome devil—cute as a pet fox, if a body remembered such creatures were not to be trusted—but now that Candie had been alerted to the danger, Max felt less uneasy about allowing the girl to indulge in a bit of a flirt with the man—broaden her education, so to speak.

Tony relaxed a bit, letting out the breath he just then realized he had been holding. The sight of Maximilien's broad grin restored both his faith in his fellow human beings and his firm belief that he was not to be denied a rewarding romantic interlude with Candie. "The hamper contains just a few trifles I asked my butler to gather from the kitchens—and the cellar, of course. My humble way of wishing you welcome to our fair city."

Max permitted a bit of his quick intelligence to show in the look he directed at the ingratiating Marquess before lowering his eyelids to mask his true feelings. "Your ducks must surely be laying, my lord, if you can call this bounty a trifle," he supplied with the promptness of the greedy, allowing his lordship to believe the worst of him. Always give the customer what he wants, Maximilien P. Murphy believed, and then feel free to take what *you* want in return.

If Tony Betancourt wanted to see Max as an opportunist who would look the other way while his lordship took liberties with his only niece, then who was Max to disappoint such a self-assured fellow? The fact that the man had about as much chance of bedding Candie as England had of seeing another Catholic monarch—especially now that Max had put his niece on her guard—would remain a private joke that Max would savor later over a glass or two of the Marquess's fine Irish whiskey.

So thinking, Max was quick to agree to Tony's suggestion that Candie accompany him on an outing through the Park, shooing them with a cheery "away with you now" as Tony helped Candie into her stylish, Wedgwood-blue pelisse, careful not to let his hands linger on her delectable shoulders.

After tying the ribbons of her matching bonnet so that the bow nestled fetchingly beneath her left ear, Candie dropped a kiss on her uncle's thatch of thick reddish-brown hair and turned to the Marquess. "Let us be off, my lord," she said, smiling cheekily, "before my uncle succumbs to temptation and dumps the hamper on the floor at your feet to begin his inventory of its contents. And a sad sight it is, don't you know, to see avarice the likes of his."

In answer to her teasing, Max reached a hand into the

hamper and came out holding a fine, plump orange, which he immediately tossed at his niece. She fielded it neatly before handing it to the Marquess. "You see, your lordship?" she told him, only a slight warning tone in her voice. "You have to be very quick if you plan to cross swords with *Uncail*."

Tony tipped his dark head to one side and looked deeply into her laughing brown eyes. "And if I wish to indulge in a little lighthearted flirting with his niece?" he prompted softly, so only she could hear.

Candie grinned, showing her white teeth to advantage. "Ah, my lord, for that you must be *very* quick indeed." Retrieving the orange from his lordship's hand, she turned toward the door before, without a word of warning, she sent the orange winging back toward Tony as he followed in her wake.

The orange narrowly missed the tip of his nose as it went singing by, only to be snatched from the air by Max, who snared it almost negligently while he pulled the cork of the whiskey bottle with his teeth.

Tony favored Candie with a deep bow. "I see I must be on my guard, madam. However, I will wager you that you will not catch me napping again."

The door closed behind them as Max was still offering his lordship very insulting odds on just such a wager.

Chapter Three

IT WAS, as the Marquess had assured her, a perfect day for a drive. There was a bit of a breeze, enough to keep the air fresh and clean, but not too strong as to wreak havoc with her bonnet and carefully casual hairstyle. The Park, always beautiful, was in exemplary form, the vivid colors of fall banishing thoughts of the damp, cold winter on its way.

Of course, sitting up behind the Marquess's perfectly matched bays and beside the handsomest man in all England had not a little to do with Candie's enjoyment of the scenery. How very nice, how perfectly lovely it was to tool along the tree-lined avenues with such a companion.

Almost, if a woman tried with all of her might, she could believe that the fairy tale could be transformed to reality. How very right, how very natural she felt in her role of society miss. The fact that she could probably outride, outshoot, outtalk, and, perhaps, outwit the Marquess —and worse yet, the fact that she might yet have to do any or all of the aforementioned—served to throw a bit of a damper on her enjoyment, but Candie had long since learned to relish the good times while they lasted and not concentrate too heavily on the future.

Out of the corner of his eye Tony watched the varying emotions come and go on Candie's face and wondered just what she was thinking. After indulging in several minutes of lighthearted banter, she had lapsed into silence a few minutes after entering the Park, and now he felt reluctant to interrupt her thoughts.

The girl was, he was finding out, composed of a series of contradictions. She had the scruples of a cardsharp, the tongue of either an Irish peasant or a titled gentlewoman, the manners of both a hoyden and a grande dame, and the sort of sharp wit that could dare to cross swords with anyone from the sarcastic Brummell to the condescending Countess Lieven. And the morals of—Ah, that was the rub. Was she a fine-boned Hariette Wilson, courtesan par excellence, or, unbelievably, a sheltered paradox who was a seasoned citizen of the world, yet unschooled in the delights of the flesh?

A sudden lift in the breeze sent a lock of Candie's baby-soft white-blonde hair to dancing against his cheek, and he caught the aroma of violets as it tickled his nostrils with the age-old scent of innocence. When he reached up a hand to brush the hair away, his fingers lingered in the tangle of soft, warm curls, and he was hard-pressed not to bring them to his lips where he could savor their sweetness.

The fact that his horses were slowing intruded on Candie's thoughts—just then centering on the story of Cinderella and casting herself in the lead—causing her to turn her head and inquire if something was amiss, thereby catching his lordship in the act of coveting his companion's hair. "Oh!" she exclaimed, hastily extracting the last errant strands from Tony's fingers. "Please forgive me, your lordship. I know it's dreadfully in the way, this wild mane of mine, but Max refuses utterly whenever I suggest having it cut off. It would be less of a trial if it were a more ordinary color—for whoever heard of white hair on a girl my age, besides there being so very much of it. In truth, half the time I feel like Prinney's pet pony, all decked out for the fair."

If Tony had been trying to look nonchalant, Candie's words destroyed the notion. "Cut your hair?" he fairly shouted. "I absolutely forbid it!"

"Do you now?" Candie purred, her spirits always enlivened by the thought of a good argument. "And who might you be to be giving me orders?"

Tony belatedly found his composure, something he lost so rarely he had little experience in having to carry on without it. Inclining his head in her direction, he apologized smoothly, "Forgive me, Miss Murphy. I presumed on our rather unique acquaintance, hoping that, having served as your rescuer yesterday, I might ask a favor in return. Cut that glorious hair if you so desire, only promise me you will not discard whatever you remove. Give it to me instead, so that I may honor it with a proper burial."

This piece of absurdity was too much for Candie. *"Bury it?"* she repeated, shocked. "It wouldn't be that you were after sampling a bit of Irish whiskey yourself before choosing a suitably fine sort to bribe Max with, would it?"

But inspiration had hit Tony and he would not be sidetracked by her attempt to draw him into defending himself. Heaving a world-weary sigh, he lent his attention to his horses for a moment—although they were a well-behaved pair and there was little traffic on the path—before shaking his head sadly and asking, "Is it so absurd to honor the demise of a part of oneself? You must have lived with that hair for quite some time, and it seems churlish to just toss it away like yesterday's *Times.*"

Trying hard not to smile, Candie asked him if he had any suggestions as to how to dispose of "the deceased."

"As a matter of fact, Candie, I do," Tony replied, using her name quite naturally; so naturally, that she could not bring herself to reprimand him for his informality. "Not that mine is an original idea, for it is the Marquess of Anglesey we have to thank for both the sensitivity and the ingenuity he employed after Waterloo when it became necessary to find something to do with the leg he had lost in battle."

"You find me utterly at your feet begging for an explanation," Candie admitted, wondering just what the soldier had contrived, not to mention how he had maintained the sangfroid that would allow him to even think overmuch of such a distressing dilemma.

Tony turned his horses so that they could make yet another turn about the circuit. "Without dressing the thing up in fine linen, the Marquess commissioned his severed leg to be put in a coffin and buried right at Waterloo. And then," he went on, throwing Candie a quick, assessing look that assured him she was more enthralled than appalled (unlike any debutante, or several matrons he could think of), "he had a headstone carved with an epitaph of his own devising. Would you care to hear the inscription?"

Candie most definitely cared to hear it, and so she told him. So while the sun shone down brightly on the scene, and while the two young people rode on through the Park, oblivious of passersby, Tony recited the words he had learned by heart:

"'Here rests—and let no saucy knave
Presume to sneer and laugh,
To learn that mouldering in the grave
Is laid—a British calf.

A leg and foot, to speak more plain
Rest here of one commanding
Who though his wits he may retain
Lost half his under-standing.

And now in England, just as gay
As in the battle brave,
He goes to rout, review and play,
With one foot in the grave.'"

"Bravo!" Candie fairly shouted, clapping her hands. "Bravo, and well done for the Marquess of Anglesey! I vow I'd love to meet the author of such a work. What a rare and levelheaded man to take a tragedy and turn it into a victory."

Tony was delighted with her instant realization that the Marquess was a man of unusual fortitude. "Ah yes, Candie, I agree," he told her before giving way to a deep sigh. "But I fear I cannot dare to top the man with any epitaph that would do credit to the glory that is your hair. My talents, such as they are, owe more to sad rehashings of someone else's words rather than the creation of my own."

"Indeed, and what, pray, could you ever find to rhyme with Murphy, in any case?" Candie laughed, gifting him with a commiserating pat on the arm. "But now that you have put the idea in my head, I believe I shall refuse to cut so much as a single hair until I can find someone who can pen a suitably fitting epitaph. You have spoiled me for less than a Byronic sonnet, I fear. But what of this talk of rehashing another's words? I confess I do not understand exactly what you mean."

The Marquess was about to do something entirely out of character: tell a woman about his little-known penchant for rewriting plays and other works of literature, satirizing them unmercifully for the amusement of his selected group of listeners. That everyone who heard his work read aloud thought him to be brilliant he disregarded as the mouthings of half-drunk lords who couldn't tell a well-turned phrase from a well-cooked cabbage, only made his sudden need to share his scribbling with Candie seem even more outlandish.

But just as he was about to speak, Candie spied a well-sprung high-perch phaeton approaching, its female driver appearing to be in the control of her team rather than the other way around. "Oh dear," Candie exclaimed, watching worriedly as the driver put the reins into one hand so that she, silly woman that she must be, could wave to the Marquess with the other. "I don't know if your lordship charts his future by the stars, but I do believe I see a meeting with a buxom, dark-haired beauty in your near future," she said, tilting her head in the direction of the oncoming equipage.

"Oh, my God," Mark Antony Betancourt groaned, dropping his chin onto his chest, "it's m'sister!"

Candie took another, longer peek at the harassed-looking woman. She saw a deliciously decorated widget whose buttercup-yellow driving ensemble was as fashionable as it was unsuitable for its intended use, her lovely, heart-shaped face nearly overwhelmed by a melting pair of wide cobalt-blue eyes—a face that mirrored a mind filled with every virtue save intelligence. *"That's* Cleopatra?" she asked incredulously. "One look at her and the asp would have begged forgiveness and committed suicide rather than harm a hair on her head. I cannot believe you two are related."

Tony was in a quandary. Introducing your sister to your light-o'-love—even if that title was just a tad premature—was simply not done. Yet if he were to turn his horses, something he should have done the moment he spied Patsy coming toward him, he would never hear the end of it, for his sister would be bound to punish him with yet another rambling lecture on the wickedness of his ways, his duty to start his nursery—a *legitimate* nursery—and the folly of associating with females from which he could conceivably "catch something." In the end, he was forced to take a deep breath, stand his ground, and take his medicine like a man.

"There's no way out of this one," he hissed in an aside

to Candie as he pasted a stiff smile on his face and waved to his sister. "If you promise not to play pranks like a hoyden—introducing yourself as Princess Candlelabra of Lamppost or some such rot—we might just brush through this without any complications."

Candie immediately took umbrage, and rightly so. Hadn't she been educated—under various names—at a succession of the best schools Max could finagle her into? What did the Marquess think she was about to do—haul out a racily decorated snuffbox and offer his sister a dip? "I do believe I can behave circumspectly, if only for the few moments it will take you to warn your sister off. After all, we wouldn't want her sensibilities unduly overset, would we," she said coldly, causing Tony to mentally kick himself for his deplorable turn of phrase.

"Don't poker up on me, Candie," he implored, still holding firm on his stiff smile. "I just meant that it would be hard for anyone to withstand the urge to run a rig on such a gullible puss as Patsy. Lord knows *I've* succumbed to the temptation more than once."

And then, before Candie could ease his apprehension by voicing her forgiveness or dash his hopes forever with a crushing setdown, Patsy hauled her team to an ungraceful halt beside his curricle, and all his energies were concentrated on simply getting out of the business with his skin intact.

"Oh, hold still, you ridiculous beasts," pleaded Lady Cleopatra Charmian Montague in her rather high, childish voice. After staring intently at her team's still occasionally quivering backs for a few reassuring moments, she turned and directed her next words to her patiently waiting brother. "Really, Antony, you'd think Harry would have had better sense than to have purchased such a high-strung pair for his own wife."

"Harry didn't buy those nags, Patsy," her sibling reminded her cordially. "He won them at Faro the week before your birthday and, ever one to take advantage of a kind providence, he immediately saw it as a sign that you were meant to receive those stupid, showy plugs for your very own. But Harry's been underground for nearly two years, pet. Surely you couldn't hurt his feelings by selling that pair before their shenanigans result in having you planted next to the old boy sooner than any of us would like."

Patsy looked past her brother, shaking her head sorrowfully as she turned to his companion for support against this crass male. "My stars, have you ever heard such hardheartedness?" she asked Candie, who was just then inspecting Lady Cleopatra's magnificent bosom and wondering why the Lord in His wisdom had chosen to give so much bounty to others and so little to herself.

"Lord Coniston shows an amazing lack of sensibility, madam, I agree," Candie responded lightly, seeing the sparkle in the other woman's eyes that clearly showed she was not adverse to his teasing. "I can only offer you my condolences in being saddled with such a brother."

Patsy Montague leaned sideways on her seat, the better to see the young woman who had spoken, for although her blue eyes were very ornamental, they were also a bit shortsighted. "Antony!" she ordered. "Introduce me to this astute young person at once. It is prodigiously refreshing to find a female who refuses to drool all over your ridiculous self-importance."

The Marquess quickly effected the introductions, passing lightly on the subject of where he had encountered Candie in the first place. "Her uncle, Maximilien P. Murphy—of the Donegal Murphys, you know—is an old acquaintance. He and his niece are ensconced on Half Moon Street for a short time between his, er, *diplomatic* engagements."

Patsy Montague didn't care a snap what Uncle Maximilien did. She sensed a romance in the air and was already deciding whether or not the *Eighth* Marquess of Coniston would inherit enough of his father's countenance to be able to withstand taunts about his ridiculous white-blonde hair, what with Eton schoolboys being so quick to taunt their mates.

"I'm so delighted to make your acquaintance, Miss Murphy," Patsy enthused, jerking on the reins and setting her restless pair to prancing. "But it is impossible to carry on a decent conversation while Harry's nags insist on fretting like this. Antony simply must bring you to dinner tomorrow night. You and your uncle, of course."

Tony's groan was audible. It was also the single inducement that he could have offered to convince Candie to accept her ladyship's invitation. "My uncle and I would be delighted, madam," she replied, avoiding Tony's speaking eyes, which at the moment were giving voice to entire volumes, all of them centering on the silent plea: Refuse her! Refuse her!

"I don't believe I'll be available tomorrow, Patsy," the Marquess said, inspiration rather than regret in his tone. "As a matter of fact, I'm sure I'm not. I'm promised to Hugh and Will for tomorrow."

His sister dismissed this slight problem with a toss of her head. "Piffle! If the day ever comes when Hugh Kinsey or Will Merritt turn down a chance to slide their legs beneath my dining table—now that I've stolen Lady Forsythe's French chef from her—I'd know the both of them to have completely lost their senses. Bring them along, Antony. You know I like your friends."

As if they had been conjured up out of a magic hat, the two gentlemen cantered up to the sitting equipages, having been in the Park exercising their mounts. Patsy espied them first, and before Tony could warn his friends off, she had both presented her invitation and acknowledged their eager acceptances.

"Now I know how a condemned man looks," Candie whispered to Tony in an aside before smiling up prettily at the two gentlemen who were staring at the Marquess, waiting to be introduced to his companion. "Take a stern grip on yourself, my lord. I do believe you are about to launch the Donegal Murphys into polite society."

It was not quite three of the clock when the Marquess of Coniston entered White's, so that the bow window set, including Lord Alvanley, John Mills, the Duke of Argyll, and the rest of that select inner circle had not yet arrived for their daily stint of ridiculing passersby through the panes with their cutting wit, in the best tradition of their departed friend and mentor, George Brummell. More than once, the Marquess had been asked to join the gentlemen, but that was not why he had come to the club this day.

Tony had made a dead set at White's directly after depositing a still maddeningly amused Miss Murphy on Half Moon Street, intent on confronting Messrs. Kinsey and Merritt and demanding they send round their regrets to his sister for the next day's dinner. After all, he thought with uncharacteristic concern for the proprieties, entertaining common criminals in one's sister's house was just not done. Once shed of Hugh and Will, he could then concentrate his efforts on dissuading the Murphys from attending as well.

He found his two friends in one of the side rooms, heatedly debating the merits of Edward Hughes Ball Hughes's latest sartorial adventure.

"I say he's still a demned fine-looking man, no matter how high his shirt-points," Mr. Hugh Kinsey was saying just as Tony entered the room.

"Rubbish," Mr. William Merritt countered. "Man walks like he's swallowed a kitchen poker; completely throws off the cut of his jacket. Divorced, you know."

"What has that got to do with anything?" Hugh retorted, throwing down his napkin in disgust. "If one limited his friends to those who weren't divorced—or just acting like it—the clubs would soon be blackballing everyone from Prinney on down. Course, then again, that mightn't be such a bad idea."

"Here, here, chaps," Tony called from the doorway, "cease this bickering before one of you ends up calling the other out. Golden Ball would have to come witness the event only because others might consider it the fashion, and Prinney would insist on being Will's second, a thought too ludicrous to contemplate. Besides," he ended, pulling out a chair and straddling it backward, "I have a boon to ask of you both."

"If it has anything to do with staying away from your sister's tomorrow so as not to cut you out with that delicious-looking morsel you was squiring in the Park earlier, *I'll* call *you* out," Will asserted quickly. "And with Hugh here wearing his heart on his sleeve for Lady Cleo this past year or more, I doubt he'll bow out gracefully either."

"Will, you amaze me," Tony said, shaking his head. "I don't know how you did it, but you came up with the correct answer—although you missed by a long chalk when it comes to the reason. It seems, you see, that I have become the unwitting tool in having m'sister stumble into inviting two common thieves to Grosvenor Square."

The hubbub that followed this calm announcement had heads turning all over the room, and Tony was forced to promise to tell all before Will, in his agitation, did himself an injury. Hugh, however, being older and therefore less prone to hysterical outbursts, had only muttered, "For shame, Antony, foisting thieves on that sweet angel," before sitting back in his chair, shaking his head. "I don't believe a word of it."

Tony told his tale over more than a few shared glasses of wine, his re-creation of Maximilien P. Murphy as a king among connivers losing nothing in the telling, but merely skimming over Candie's participation as being no more than a sad consequence of being thrust into her uncle's care. He was already more than half on his way to believing this to be the true way of things, his impression clouded only by Candie's seeming enjoyment of her role.

37

"The Maharajah of Budge-Budge?" Hugh said wonderingly once Tony had signaled the end of his little story by taking a long swallow from his glass. "And you mean to tell me the constable swallowed such a thin tale? It doesn't say much for the caliber of our London law officers, does it."

But while Hugh's logical mind was hard pressed to believe his fellow man's gullibility, Will had taken another tack. He was more than a little impressed, by both Uncle Max and his beautiful niece, and declared that he couldn't wait to sit down to dinner with such an interesting couple.

"But, don't you see, you clothhead," the Marquess was harried into declaring, "the entire purpose of telling you about the Murphys was so that you would have the good sense to *avoid* them. And to have them in m'sister's house —why, she'd never forgive me once she found out the truth about them."

Hugh, older than his friend by some half dozen years, inspected the Marquess at length before speaking. "Tony, old fellow," he said at last, "I do believe you are protesting overmuch. After all, you are still the same Mark Antony Betancourt who brought a lion cub—and not a bit housebroken as I recall—to your sister's dress ball three Seasons past, are you not? And the same Mark Antony Betancourt who talked that same sister into allowing herself to be rolled up in a dusty old rug for the masquerade this past Yuletide—and then unrolled her in front of a roomful of people to find she had dressed only in her underclothing as it was so warm inside the rug? Really, I find it hard to believe you are suddenly under acute attack from your conscience just because Cleo's invited a pair of gay adventurers to dine a single time."

Will narrowed his eyes and looked at Tony intently. "Yes, dear Hugh, you're right. It does seem rather out of character. Perhaps our good friend has designs on the lady in question. We did both comment that she was a fine-looking female. But really, Tony, Hugh's already spoken for—what with him drooling over your sister—and I've got more than I can handle just now with Tilly. Covent Garden Warblers aren't coming cheap this year, you know."

"Then you refuse to stand by me in this?" Tony asked dramatically. "You refuse to save my sister from possible embarrassment?"

"Actually, old chap," Hugh contradicted smoothly, "it is you we refuse to aid. But we are all eagerness to witness your rescue attempts. Such brotherly concern is so affecting, don't you know?"

Tony rose from his chair in disgust. "I knew I could count on my oldest and dearest friends," he said waspishly. "All right, gentlemen. I shall handle the situation myself. Just don't say I didn't warn you." Just before he quit the room, he turned to his friends, adding in awful tones, "And if you're smart, gentlemen, you will keep your purses close to your chests!"

When Max returned from a leisurely stroll about town —just checking up on his old friends and favorite haunts —it was to the sight of his niece curled up in a comfortable chair near the front window, busily mending a slight tear in his blue satin "ambassador" breeches while humming a happy, if somewhat ribald, Irish ditty beneath her breath.

"Ah, m'darling girl, and how goes the siege?" he asked, dropping a light kiss on her blonde head.

"The castle walls are still standing strong, *Uncail,* while the attacking force is rapidly being deserted by his allies, who one by one seem to be coming over to our side," Candie told him, a smile of unholy glee lighting her face. "Tell me, my dear Mr. Murphy, are you agreeable to dining tomorrow night with the Queen of the Nile?"

Chapter Four

"HOLD THERE a moment, Mr. Murphy!"

Max's posture stiffened a moment, expecting the law to swoop down momentarily and clap him on the shoulder, before turning neatly on his heels to take in the sight of Lord Coniston bearing down on him.

"I thought I might find you here on Bond Street this morning, sir, seeing as how your niece said you spend your idle hours inspecting public buildings."

Not appreciating his lordship's witticism even a little bit, Max pasted a false smile on his face and said, "And the top of the morning to you, my lord. And are you an insulting man by nature or have you sharpened your tongue especially for Maximilien P. Murphy?"

Falling into step beside the older man, Tony hastily apologized for his words, explaining that as the term was new to him, he had been itching to use it on someone. "I have studied many forms of speech, Mr. Murphy," the

Marquess said, "but so far the intricacies of Irish–English remain a mystery. I must say I am quite intrigued."

"Hummph" was all that Max replied. "And now, my lord, now that you consider your bread well buttered, what is it you'd be wanting from me this morning? And make no mistake, laddie, if you're thinking what I think you're thinking, for a friend that can be bought is not worth the buying."

Tony stopped in his tracks, looking highly affronted. "I resent that remark, Mr. Murphy," he fairly growled. "I know that I have detected a want of openness in our short acquaintance, but if you sincerely believe that I would be so crass as to sink to *buying* your favor—for some obscure reason—then I do believe we have no more to say to each other." And Lord Coniston turned on his heels, about to depart the scene.

"I'll tell my niece you've said goodbye," Max said off-handedly, causing Tony to halt in his tracks. "Ah-ha!" he went on triumphantly. "Just as I thought. You love me, boyo, like the Devil loves holy water. But m'niece is a different kettle of fish, isn't she? Well let me give you another bit of speech particular to the Irish—I swear by all that's holy that if you harm a single hair on Candie's fair head I'll hang a piece of you on every lamppost in London, and no mistake."

Tony immediately, and with some heat, denied that he had any but the kindest, most altruistic thoughts about Candice Murphy, a calumny that may have rolled off his tongue with easy fluency but not without some pain to his basic sense of decency, rarely used but still functioning. "Mr. Murphy, you have told me yourself that you have been traveling about with Miss Murphy since she was little more than a baby. But now she is a woman grown, as you well know. This vagabond life you lead is no life for a gently nurtured female, for I am not so blind as to overlook the fact that somewhere along the line Miss Murphy has had the benefit of fine English schooling. I cannot in good conscience turn my back on the poor girl now that I have met her. I swear to you sir, I have only Miss Murphy's best interests at heart."

Max tucked his hand around his lordship's elbow and urged the younger man to walk on with him a bit. "What you are saying then, my lord, is that we are both on the same side, both of us looking to Candie's best interests," he said, putting the Marquess once again at his ease. "But I ask you, sir? Have you never heard of Lord Thomond's cocks?"

Tony smiled. "Why do I feel that once again I'm going to be taken to the fair? All right, Max, I'll bite. Tell me about Lord Thomond's cocks."

Max let go his grip on his lordship in order to rub his palms together reflectively as they sauntered along Bond Street. "Well, laddie, it seems Lord Thomond had hired himself an Irish cock-feeder. Not only had he hired him, but he entrusted him with his prize cocks, cocks which were matched for a considerable sum the next day. But when his lordship showed up in the morning to claim his animals, he found that they were all either lamed or dead. And you'll be wanting to know the reason for this phenomenon? Well, so did Lord Thomond, and no mistake! He asked his Irish cock-feeder what the devil had happened, and the man replied, a perplexed look on his freckled face, 'I don't know what happened, your lordship. I shut them up all right and tight together in the one room, figuring as how they were all your cocks, all on the same side, so to speak, they would not disagree.'"

"You're saying you and I might disagree about what is best for your niece?" Tony asked, as he knew he was supposed to do.

"I believe your idea of what's best for my Candie owes much to what you think is best for yourself, my lord, if you catch my meaning."

"And what about you, Max?" Tony countered, flushing

a bit. "Aren't you likewise guilty of using Candie to your own purposes?"

"Ah, you slipped there, laddie," Max pointed out. "You called my niece 'Candie.' A bit of a warning, boyo. In Ireland, *candy* means to be drunk. Careful you don't start getting light-headed on thoughts of my Candie, for she's not for you."

Now this last statement of Max's put the man firmly where Tony wanted him, for hadn't he sought the fellow out with the intention of appealing to the man's better nature, convincing him that it would be the height of folly to show up at Lady Montague's that evening? Yet, strangely, Tony found that he could not bring himself to take advantage of the opening he had been granted.

It was a terrible war that raged within the handsome breast of the Marquess of Coniston. Part of him, the protective-brother part, could find no rationale to explain foisting two con artists off as respectable citizens worthy of sitting down to supper with his one and only sibling. But another, baser part of him could only stand back and whisper in his ear, "And who would be the wiser if Max and Candie could pull off another of their impersonations?"

Besides, it rankled that Max suspected a peer of the realm of ulterior motives. Not that it wasn't true, of course, but who was Max to say so aloud? Being a woman of indeterminate background, Candie was fair game, wasn't she? If I turn Max against me now, Tony thought irritably, I will have lost any chance of seeing Candie again, for she will not disobey her uncle. Yet if I sanction launching the two bogus Murphys into polite society, it will put Candie on a par with any other society miss, subject to only the most tame courting.

"What do you want from me?" the Marquess finally asked, having totally defeated himself with his own logic.

Once again Max took his companion's arm. "I knew you were an intelligent fellow, my lord, from the moment I first clapped eyes on you. You were right, too, about my

Candie being a gently nurtured female, not that she isn't always awake to what's trumps, as I've made sure to give her a well-rounded education. But she'll be reaching her majority soon, as you yourself pointed out, and it isn't much longer that I can have the child frolicking about the countryside with me without the poor dear coming to harm. But if I could see her launched into society, only in a small way, you understand, perhaps a fine young man will take her to wife and keep her safe. Your sister, my lord, may be just the ticket, don't you know."

Tony's mind was muddled, but it had not yet entirely ceased to function. "Why don't you just hire yourselves one of those female dragons as chaperone and launch her yourself? Surely that can't be so hard—not for the grand Maharajah of Budge-Budge?"

Max just shook his head. "I thought of doing it m'self, but Candie will have none of it. Seems the gel's taken it in her head never to marry. Some farradiddle about not landing some poor innocent with a female of no background. I swear on m'mother's eyes, I don't know where the child goes to come up with such ideas. We Murphys were Kings once, you know." His little outburst over, Max waved a pudgy hand in dismissal of Candie's sensibilities on the subject and went on. "But if your sister were to take her up, as I said before, only in a small way, Candie would be seen by the eligible bachelors still in town. And I'd not be bragging to say it's many a heart will be hers for the asking, and with the little dear none the wiser that she's fallen in with my scheme."

"And what of Lady Montague's reputation once it is found out she foisted off an imposter as a well-bred young lady? After all, even though m'sister is a sad racket herself, being a widow and having a bit more latitude in her actions, she would be pushed completely beyond the pale once the truth were known."

Max smiled slightly. The fact that his lordship had not turned down his suggestion out of hand showed that there was hope for an amicable solution. "If that day ever comes, and I doubt it will, for I say to you now with all modesty that having won my Candie in matrimony, no man would even think to cry foul over such a trifling incidental. And if he does, then of course I, Maximilien P. Murphy, will stand up straight and tall and name myself as the sole instigator of the scheme."

"If we can find you," the Marquess muttered under his breath. "And what am I to get from all this, Max?" Tony asked, suddenly realizing Candie was slipping through his fingers and into a world that would find him no closer to bedding her than if she had been transported posthaste to the far side of the moon.

Max stopped dead in his tracks and favored his lordship with an incredulous look. "What would you have to gain, my lord? Why, you disappoint me, and no mistake. What I offer you in exchange for your help with Candie is, and I do not offer it lightly, the benefit of my years of experience in dealing with my fellow man. It's an education all your fine name and money cannot buy for you, for it must be either learned on the streets or not learned at all. Here I stand, ready to divulge the secret of reading human character, and you dare to ask 'What's in it for me?' By the saints, man, I took you to be smarter than that."

The older man had succeeded in making Tony smile. "And what is it you could be teaching me, Max? How to dress like an Italian Count? How to shimmy down tied bedsheets to avoid the innkeeper?"

But Max was not upset by the Marquess's teasing words. Looking about him, he espied a group of workmen standing idle on the kerb, shovels and pickaxes hanging idly at their sides. "Do you, for instance, know that you English obey anyone who appears to be in charge, never asking a single question as to right or wrong, just so long as the person in charge acts like he knows what he is about?"

"That's preposterous," Tony denied hotly. "Englishmen are renowned for thinking for themselves."

"Oh, really?" Max had a gleam in his eyes that had Tony leaning closer to him to catch his next words. "Supposing I was to tell you that I could get those workmen over there to follow my orders just by acting like I was a person of authority? Would it be worth a monkey to prove my theory wrong?"

"You're already floating badly downstream in River Tick, Max," Tony challenged. "Where would you get the blunt to pay me if you're wrong?"

Once again Max smiled, a sweet, Irish, cherubic smile. "And don't you know it's the Irish who invented the IOU? Besides, I won't lose, my lord. You will, and no mistake. Tell you what, though, just to sweeten the pot a bit for you—how about I make a further condition? If I win, you agree to have your sister sponsor my Candie. If I lose, I'll give you two clear weeks to seduce m'niece without ever so much as blinking. Here," he said, holding out his hand, "I give you my hand and my word on it."

Tony looked across the way at the workmen, still standing about idly, and then back at Maximilien P. Murphy, grinning like a bear as he stood there, hand outstretched. "It's a deal!" the Marquess said, already mentally planning his assault on Candie's virtue.

After admonishing the Marquess to stand back out of the way—so as not to influence the workmen's decision by his presence—Max sauntered over to the laborers, his malacca cane swinging idly from his hand. Unerringly approaching the workman who looked to him to be the most intelligent of the crew, Max halted, spread his legs ever so slightly, and puffed out his chest. "And is this what you are paid good money to do, mister, stand about with your thumb up your—"

The precise positioning of the workman's thumb was left to Tony's imagination as Max's loud bellow lowered to a fierce growl. The harassed laborer's muffled protestations and wild hand wavings were mimicked beautifully by Max, who even went so far as to pull some official-looking documents from his pocket and brandish them in the workman's face.

Tony could see the exact second when the workman's attitude changed from one of belligerence to subservience. He and his fellows then listened attentively for a few minutes while Max instructed them before setting to with a will, wielding their shovels and pickaxes in what seemed like an unnecessarily violent violation of Bond Street's smooth surface.

"What on earth did you say to them?" the Marquess asked as Max, his cane twirling in slow, graceful circles within his talented fingers, joined him again on the flagway.

"And you'll be wanting to know all my secrets at one go, laddie?" Max said with a wink. "I'll tell you this and nothing more: I, Mr. Edward Q. Davison, architectural engineer to his royal majesty, have just taken the first step in carrying out my latest commission—digging a trench, two feet wide by three feet in depth, from this side of Bond Street to the other. My workmen, as you can see, are putting to with a will, having been duly impressed with my written orders and, as I told you earlier, by the mere fact that Englishmen are sheep—easily led by anyone who appears to know what he is doing."

Tony looked again toward the workmen, the length of their trench already beginning to cause a lamentable snarling of the heavy Bond Street traffic, smiled ruefully and asked, "What did you tell the workmen to do once the trench is finished?"

Busily inspecting the neat fingernails of his left hand, Max replied calmly, "Edward Q. Davison is no hard taskmaster. Once the trench is completed, the workmen are free to return to their homes, of course."

The Marquess tried hard not to laugh aloud, his quick mind already picturing the havoc Max had provoked in order to prove his point. "Max!" he exclaimed, taking a large gulp of air. "You wouldn't?"

Looking every inch a mischievous leprechaun, Maximilien P. Murphy raised one bushy eyebrow and purred, "Would a duck swim?"

Tony could no longer restrain his mirth. His explosion of laughter, hardly heard above the sound of cursing coachmen and protesting peers, rang out gaily as he clutched at his companion in order to remain upright.

"Takes the cockles off your heart, don't it, laddie?" Max said, clearly quite pleased with both himself and his bit of mischief. Slipping his hand around Tony's elbow — for it was not a wise man who stayed to watch the blaze when it was he who lit the match — the pair pushed off toward St. James's Street and the Cocoa Tree, Max saying something about mischief being thirsty work and being in need of some refreshing six and tips to wet down his dry throat.

The remainder of the afternoon passed so pleasantly, with Max regaling his young friend with ribald stories of his adventurous past, that it wasn't until Tony was dressing for dinner that he realized that, not only was he out a goodly sum of money, he had committed himself to being a co-conspirator in Max's matrimonial plans for Candie. And, he remembered, cursing violently as he ruined yet another neckcloth, he had at least temporarily scotched his own plans for making that same young lady his next mistress.

"Damned wily Bog Lander!" he swore, smiling a bit in spite of himself.

"My compliments, Tony," Hugh imparted quietly, absently twirling his wineglass. "That girl is quite the most beautiful creature I have ever seen. And not only are you the one to discover the ever so ravishing Miss Murphy, but you do it while the town is all but shut up for the impending winter. Except for Will and a half dozen or so other bucks, it would seem you're to have a clear shot at her hand. But then you always did have the Devil's own luck, didn't you?"

Tony smiled sardonically. "If Miss Murphy's hand were the portion of her glorious anatomy I had in mind, dear friend, I might be liable to agree with you. As it is, her dainty little paw is hers to bestow when and where she wishes. I'll make do with possessing the rest of her—for as long as it suits me, of course. But I notice you have not included yourself as one of Miss Murphy's possible suitors. How long do you propose to wear the willow for my scatterbrained sister before you give it up?"

Hugh Kinsey peered across the Montague drawing room at the love of his life, at the moment being entertained by one of Max Murphy's hilarious tall stories, and replied without rancor, "As long as it takes, old son, as long as it takes. I only wish you could be well and truly struck by cupid's little arrows. Perhaps then you'd show a little sympathy toward your fellow man rather than taking such obvious delight in our suffering. Oh," he added, seemingly as an afterthought, "and you can leave off spouting rubbish like some rakehell libertine—seeing as how there's none but me to hear you, and you'll never get me to believe you'd ever despoil an innocent maid. It's not your style, Tony, and we both know it. Can it be this Miss Murphy makes your to-date stone-hard heart go pitter-pat so that you need boast about your prowess in some desperate attempt to protect yourself from your finer feelings?"

"Not content to suffer only the pangs of unrequited love, Hugh, you now seem intent on pinning your hopes on impossible dreams," the Marquess responded repressively, fingering the quizzing glass that hung round his neck from a black riband. "Don't look for this particular man to ever succumb to that debilitating disease you so rashly call love. I'd just as soon put my head in a noose. Besides, I'm having entirely too much fun bedding everyone else's love. Lord, the wives in this town fairly line up for my favors. Hardly an endorsement of the institution, is it?"

"Ah, yes," Mr. Kinsey returned placidly, "your reputation, Mister Overnite, is, I'm sure you believe, something to be envied. But, please, do not number me among your admirers. Your easy conquests of what amount to nothing more than titled jades has given you a jaundiced attitude I do not envy, although I am glad you restrict your affairs to women of the world and leave the innocents to their virginal dreams." Looking once again at the beauteous Miss Murphy as she sat demurely listening to Lady Montague describing her latest purchase—a particularly outrageous red velvet-trimmed bonnet—Hugh ventured idly, "Miss Murphy is not your usual flirt, Tony, not by a long chalk, although I can easily see she is not the usual milk and water debutante either. If she's a thief, she's a *chaste* thief. She is clearly ineligible for seduction, no matter what the sins of her uncle. Strange. For if you are not bamming me, your pursuit of her does not stem from any thought of finally setting up your nursery, and I'm sure as I am of my love for your sister, you're after the chit. This gets curiouser and curiouser, old man, as you can't have it both ways. Perhaps you should dismiss the girl from your mind entirely and get back to the business of cuckolding every second husband in England."

His dark eyes flashing with suppressed fury, Tony retorted in a fierce undertone, "Don't push too hard, Hugh. Anyone would think you've set yourself up as Miss Murphy's protector. Believe me, it's not necessary. Her uncle is formidable enough to keep me from ravishing the chit here in m'sister's house like some bloody rutting boar. Oh yes, I admit to lusting after the dear Miss Murphy— what man could overlook such a fetching piece of goods? —but even I have more scruples than to ruin an innocent girl. The thing is, Hugh," he began confidentially, "I'm positive Miss Murphy ain't—"

Tony hadn't seen the butler enter the room and nod to Lady Montague, who then hopped spritely to her feet and announced, "Dinner is served, my dears. Hurry do, as

Louis so abominates it when his creations are left standing for so much as a moment."

Patsy, taking Max as her partner, led the way to the dining room, commanding her brother to assist Miss Murphy while winking broadly at Hugh and Will and teasing them as to who should take whose arm as the two gentlemen brought up the rear.

It was an informal dinner, with Lady Montague at one end of the table and the Marquess at the other, the Murphys to Tony's right, and the single gentlemen to his left as they sat around the table in the smaller, family dining room.

"I had Soames remove that great hulking silver centerpiece Lord Montague's mother cursed us with so that we would be able to talk across the table without craning our necks like agitated storks. After all, how are people supposed to become acquainted if they are limited to speaking only with the persons to their immediate right or left? I cannot begin to tell you the number of crushing bores I've had to endure at formal dinner parties. This is cozier, don't you think, Miss Murphy?"

Tony had been forestalled in his intention of warning Hugh yet again about the Murphys (and thereby justifying his seemingly indecent designs on Candie's person), giving him a moment or two to rethink his motives for continuing to insist his new acquaintances were the basest of frauds. Instead, he had decided to leave their final judgment to Hugh and Will themselves, telling himself his was an academic exercise meant to discover both the extent of his friends' gullibility and the magnitude of the Murphys' talent to deceive.

His decision did not, however, extend to lending the Murphys a helping hand in their deception. To this end, he cleared his throat slightly and inclined his head in Candie's direction. "Yes, Miss Murphy," he prodded facetiously, "do let us hear your opinion on the subject. For one so well traveled, I'm sure you've had occasion to sit through many a formal dinner in any number of countries, dealing with all the customs peculiar to each nationality."

Candice, her sherry eyes sparkling as she looked the Marquess square in his handsome, grinning face—telling him without words that she knew just what he was about —readily took up the challenge. "I have found formal dining to be much the same everywhere on the Continent, although I will say that I have never seen such a fuss as I did when we dined with her highness in Sweden. Of course, the Spanish and the Italians are no slouches when it comes to fanfare, with small armies of servants parading in the courses as if each silver platter bore its own holy grail. As to the customs in Africa, I'm afraid I must refer you to my uncle, as I dined in seclusion with the women while the Emir entertained Max with scantily clad dancing girls as they partook of nasty-looking stuffed grape leaves and honey cakes."

Max took up where Candie left off—not requiring the none too gentle cue she sent him by way of a swift kick on the shin—and re-created the scene inside the unidentified Emir's enormous red-and-white striped tent in his own inimitable style.

After describing some of the more bizarre foods that were served—causing Will Merritt to completely lose his appetite for the poached salmon on his plate—he went on to explain how honey cakes were made of endless paper-thin layers of pastry spread with finely chopped pistachio nuts and steeped in purest honey. "Their resulting taste is so delightful, my friends, that if the Holy Father should ever bite into one he'd outlaw the cakes as an occasion of sin, and no mistake. If you wish, Lady Montague, I'll write down the recipe for your chef. The Emir was kind enough to have his men impart it to me, seeing as how I'd done his highness a small service and he insisted on rewarding me. It was nip and tuck there for a while, making him see that I would find it difficult explaining away the three wives he wished to gift me with once I was back in

England, but I finally convinced him the recipe was payment enough."

"Max had a harder time talking the Emir into believing he was not insulting him by turning down the six camels, twelve goats, and small chest of jewels his son offered him in return for making *me* his number-one wife," Candie interjected, laughing at the memory.

"And many's the day I regret those pretty baubles slipping through my fingers," Max said, shaking his head. "But for all she can be a sore trial to me at times—nagging at me worse than a wife, don't you know—at least, as I pointed out to the Emir, I don't have to constantly remember to keep myself upwind of her."

"Oh, Mr. Murphy, surely you're bamming us," Patsy protested, lightly slapping his hand. "You'd never trade your niece for some smelly livestock and a few jewels."

"I'd trade m'sister Barbara in a minute," Will averred, reaching for his wineglass. "Wouldn't have to be a big chest of baubles neither, and that's a fact."

His plan to discommode Candice having come to nothing, Tony withdrew from the lively conversation that followed, as Max and his niece dominated the scene, answering question after question put to them by Patsy, Hugh, and the noticeably impressed Will Merritt.

It wasn't until the gentlemen had rejoined the ladies in the drawing room after port and cigars that the Marquess was able to maneuver Candice off into a corner for some private conversation.

He did not waste time complimenting her on her gown —a simply cut but stunningly attractive lime-green confection stamped with the unmistakable look of a superior Parisian modiste—but went straight to the heart of things, demanding to know what she and Max planned to do about extricating themselves from further meetings with his sister.

As Patsy had already invited the two of them to a card party she was holding the following Monday evening (while Tony had cringed inwardly at the thought of Max fuzzing the cards and dealing from the bottom of the deck), Tony could not pretend he was not upset by what was rapidly turning into a "situation."

Candie looked her adversary up and down carefully, doing her best to pass over his obvious handsomeness and concentrating on his graceless lack of faith in her ability to mix with "decent" people without either lifting the family silver or drinking from the fingerbowl, and said calmly, "Max is on vacation—a sabbatical of sorts—and not planning anything in the near future that could possibly give us away for the nasty felons that you think us to be. We're merely tourists enjoying the city for a space, my lord. Your sister and your friends are congenial company. The only pitfall in sight is your own behavior. The way you watch our every move lest we make a misstep, while at the same time trying your best to trip us up yourself, will soon cause comment if you can't bring yourself under some semblance of control.

"So I say to you, my lord," she ended, her polite, social smile never fading by so much as a hair, "either fish or cut bait. In other words, either relax and enjoy our temporary friendship or take yourself off once and for all. After all, it wasn't Max or me who came scratching at *your* door bearing gifts."

"You know damn full well why I came back," Tony hissed under his breath.

"Indeed, I do," Candice acknowledged. "You have planned to make me your mistress. Do I flatter myself? Perhaps it was just one quick toss in the hay you had in mind. I must admit the six bottles of Irish whiskey are what put me off—as it seems a trifle overdone if you were angling for merely one night of pleasure. Or am I completely wrong, my lord, and I am not the target of your attentions? Perhaps it is Uncle Max whom you wish to cultivate, just in case you ever gamble away your inheritance and needs must scramble to make your way in the world. I can see how Max's little money-making schemes would appeal much more than, say, hiring yourself out as a crossing sweep."

Tony's neck was turning a dull shade of red, so greatly did he wish to grab hold of the infuriating female before him and shake her—or kiss her—until he put a stop to her agile tongue. "I told you there were no strings attached to my gifts except for my request—I said *request*, madam— that your uncle tell me a little more about his exploits. You flatter yourself, Candie, if you think I would jeopardize my sister's reputation just for the dubious pleasure of being the latest man to share your bed. Even my interest in Max has paled, as he is, after all, no more than a glorified thief."

Candie's eyebrows rose as she acknowledged his insults. "In that case, my lord, I can see no problems left to plague you. Max won't pine away if you disappear from our lives, and your sister, charming widget that she is, will soon forget us once something else comes along to occupy her mind."

She held out her hand, and he took it automatically. "I doubt that we will be meeting again, my lord, as we don't travel in the same circles. At least not as Maximilien and Candice Murphy we don't. Thank you again for the gifts, the ride in the park, and this delightful dinner."

Before Tony could think of anything to say, Candie had rejoined her uncle, explaining that she had a slight head-ache and would like to retire. Max shot the Marquess a sharp look before acting the solicitous uncle and ushering his niece into Lady Montague's carriage for the ride back to Half Moon Street, Patsy's promise to send round an invitation to her card party speeding them on their way.

As Tony sat sprawled in one of his sister's most uncomfortable armchairs, his nose sunk deep in his brandy glass, Hugh and Will also took their leave, Will announcing that he was off to White's as it was too shockingly early to go home, and Hugh lingering interminably over Patsy's hand, giving his hostess cause to think he had put his back out and was stuck in that bent over position.

When brother and sister were finally alone, Patsy, who needed little encouragement to play matchmaker, extolled Candie's virtues in such glowing terms and at such length that Candice's fictional headache became a very real, throbbing pain in his lordship's weary brain.

"Miss Murphy is not my sort," Tony protested at last, seeing no end to Patsy's litany of praises to Candie's virtues.

"Horsefeathers," his sister sniffed, giving her dark head a toss. "Anything in skirts is your sort. I grant you I don't know how she's situated financially, but you're rich as Croesus, so that's no obstacle. And don't say she don't appeal to your eyes, for a prettier child I've yet to see, what with that glorious hair and that sweet, innocent face."

"Sweet? Innocent?" Tony barked, rising to his feet and slapping his glass down on a nearby table with considerable force before common sense (and a healthy concern for his self-preservation) intervened to stop his tirade short of giving the game away to his sister. "You know I cut a wide berth around the sweet and innocent, puss," he substituted smoothly.

Well, thought his older and sometimes wiser sibling, I can't see why he's taking *my* head off. After all, it wasn't me who found the girl, but him. If the chit hadn't caught his fancy, what was he doing driving her around the Park, he who hadn't been seen with an eligible female up beside him in more than a half dozen years? "Then why did you take her out for a drive?" she asked penetratingly.

"I did it as a favor to Max," Tony improvised hurriedly. "He felt she needed some air. In point of fact, my acquaintance is with Mr. Murphy. We, er, we have many mutual interests."

"Oh? Is he also a writer?"

As Tony's writing—or scribbling, as he chose to dismiss his satirical compositions—was one of his main interests, it seemed a good idea to agree with Patsy. "After a fashion, puss. Max and I are both students of human nature, and I value his opinions and insights. Indeed, I've already learned one lesson from him." A rather expensive lesson, he mused ruefully, remembering the thick envelope he had passed over to Max earlier in the evening. "It is my hope I can return the favor." And retrieve my blunt, he added silently.

Patsy visibly relaxed. "Then you'll be seeing Candice —I mean Max—again?"

Tony's eyes narrowed as he recalled Candie's icy dismissal. He had not changed his mind, no matter how vehemently he denied the fact to Candie—he planned to have her in his bed. Max may have gained his niece some time by winning the wager that afternoon, but tomorrow was another day and the gamester's luck couldn't hold forever.

Let the Murphys have their fun parading about in society for a space. In the end he, Mark Antony Betancourt, would triumph, of that he was as certain as he was that the sun rose in the east.

"Yes, pet, I'll be seeing the Murphys again," he assured his sister before dropping a kiss on her cheek and heading off to his own town house. "Dismiss me like some lowly lackey, will she?" he muttered to himself as his coach rolled through the darkened streets. "Hussy! And to think I had actually begun to doubt my reading of her character. I may be temporarily shackled by my wager with Max, but two weeks from today the gloves come off. I'll have my way with her before the month is out, and that conniving Irishman won't be richer for it by so much as a single flea-bitten nanny goat!"

Chapter Five

IT WAS a beautiful cradle, ornately carved and decorated with gilt and burnished gold, and sporting an ornamented canopy and chased carrying handles. Max had bought it for her, paying down the ridiculously high sum of fifty-two pounds, and Candie would no more think of parting with it than she would consider ridding herself of her right hand, even though carting it about the world in its specially constructed case was not always simple, considering their occasional hurried departures.

Candie had never slept in the cradle—a handy dresser drawer or carpet of leaves being her usual resting place as a babe—but Max had sworn his little princess deserved a cradle and, when she reached the age of ten and was long past the need for rocking, he had kept his promise.

Now, as she used a soft cloth to lovingly wipe away the dust from the intricate lion head designs that edged each rocker, Candie felt the familiar warm swell of emotion that filled her breast whenever she thought back to the day her uncle had burst through the door of the humble Irish cottage they had leased after a run of luck with the ponies, an unabashed look of pride on his face as he knelt at her feet, the cradle nestled gently in his arms.

Candie may not have known a mother's love, but she'd never felt the least bit cheated. For Candie had Max, and Max, with his great heart, constant humor, and unflagging zest for living, was all the home and family she could ever need.

Her task completed, Candie rose to her feet, wandering around the small sitting room, occasionally flicking her cloth over a table or one of the cheap knickknacks the landlord had employed to lend credence to his description of the rooms as "elegantly decorated in the first stare of fashion."

It had been three days since Lady Montague's dinner party, three long days that could not be adequately filled by shopping for foodstuffs at Covent Garden, or preparing meals, or mending clothing, or flicking nonexistent dust from inferior china vases.

Yet it was not simple boredom that had Candie spending long hours staring out the window overlooking Half Moon Street and nagging her uncle about his smelly cigars and the frequency of his medicinal doses of Irish whiskey until he clapped his hat on his head and stomped off in search of some company less liable to find fault with every breath he took.

And it was not worry over their lack of funds that made her attempts at sleep a mockery, causing her to toss and turn far into the night, punishing her pillow as she strove to find a comfortable resting place for her weary head. Not that she was ever the sort to worry overmuch about finances—that was Max's province. He "found" the money; she merely managed it.

When her uncle had tossed a thick packet of bank notes in her lap two mornings earlier, it did not occur to her to ask questions as to its origin; she merely commenced to dividing it up in her usual fashion, alloting certain amounts for food, clothing, a few luxuries, and, because she had learned early in life that her main function was to scamper dutifully along at Max's heels, sweeping up for him as he acted out his grandiose schemes, setting aside a reassuring amount in case she had either to post bail or finance a hasty disappearance.

No, there was nothing in Candie's present existence that differed in the slightest from the norm. They were resting, she and Max, taking time off from their travels and scheming to, as her uncle termed it, give their brains a holiday. But it wasn't that she was missing the rush of excitement Max's antics engendered.

What she missed was the rush of excitement *Tony's* antics—for how else could she term his behavior?—engendered. He had exploded into her life unexpectedly and uninvited, and in less than a week had shown her sides of herself she had never known existed.

She hadn't needed Max's warnings to recognize how dangerous Tony was, how potentially destructive this sophisticated man of the world could be to her emotional well-being. Mark Antony Betancourt was a wealthy, titled, highly intelligent, wildly egotistical, sexually promiscuous, mainly unprincipled, selfish, pleasure-seeking rotter of the first order.

He was also, she reminded herself on a sigh, wealthy, titled, highly intelligent, devilishly handsome, sexually devastating, oddly vulnerable, endearingly obtuse, gratifyingly loyal, and the most unbelievably exciting male she had ever met.

Candie had long ago made up her mind never to marry and followed this decision with a second determination, to go to her grave a maiden, as befitted a good Irish girl, no matter how infamous the circumstances of her birth.

Until her acquaintance with Tony Betancourt, she'd had no reason to doubt her ability to live up to her solemn vow of chastity. Yet not only did she now find herself suddenly questioning her ability to stick to her promises, but she had actually begun having dreams—most disturbing dreams—that might, she thought, shivering a bit, condemn her to eternal hellfire anyway, without ever having experienced the joy of Tony's embrace. It was highly unfair, that's what it was, she protested to her guardian angel (just then pacing back and forth atop Candie's shoulder, sighing and tsk-tsking a lot). If I'm going to burn in Hades for mere *thoughts,* I may as well do the deed. After all, a sinner is entitled to *some* pleasure, isn't she?

Planting her restless self in the chair nearest to the street, her chin cupped in her palm, she raised her left hand to push back the lace curtains in order to look down at the passersby, automatically singling out the most interesting or unique ones and studying the way they walked, the inclination of their heads, their facial expressions that revealed self-confidence, greed, anxiety, and, reflected on the countenance of one fashionably dressed maiden, barely concealed contempt for the scene around her.

Mimicking the haughty debutante's high-nosed posture, Candie folded her full pink mouth into a thin line, lowered her eyelids to half-mast, and pronounced in her best young ladies' boarding school accents, "It fatigues me beyond permission that we cannot progress more than two feet in any direction without some encroaching person accosting us just so they can later say Miss Isabel Snobface spoke with them in passing. Does not anyone know their place anymore, Reginald?"

As the young lady passed out of sight, Candie dropped her pose and looked around for another subject. Max had assigned her this exercise when she was barely old enough to walk erect, and over the course of the years she had perfected many different characterizations, both male and female, that she and Max often employed to their benefit from Genoa to Edinburgh.

A natural-born mimic, as were many Irish, Candie could readily portray anyone from a drooling imbecile to a royal

Princess without fear of discovery, and now, as she stood up and practiced the measured shuffling of a weary pie seller bent over after years of carrying his heavy tray through the streets of London, it did not occur to her that hers was an accomplishment not common to other young females.

Just as she considered herself satisfied with her impersonation, her eye was caught by the confident stride and neat figure of a lone male just then crossing the street in front of number sixty-three. What a laudable example of the "Compleat English Nobleman," she mused appreciatively, knowing that her own shorter stature and thin build made it impossible for her to ever carry such an impersonation off with the dash and flair this man possessed naturally. She made a tolerable African prince, she owned placatingly, but when it came to English lords, she limited herself to the roles of effeminate fops or out at the elbows second sons.

Her attention caught by the well-dressed gentleman, Candie abandoned her lessons for the day and, as had been the case of late, the moment her mind was unoccupied it became peopled with visions of the Marquess of Coniston, crowding her brain with images of the man as he had looked each of the three times she had been in his company. So real was her imagining that even the gentleman in the street now took on the guise of the unsettling Mark Antony.

Pushing back the curtains, she placed her hands on the windowsill and took a closer look at the man who had just reached the flagway beneath her window. "Oh dear Blessed Virgin, it *is* him!" she exclaimed, suddenly very nervous as she whirled away from the window in the hope he hadn't seen her staring down at him like some love-struck infant.

She made a mad dash to the mirror to straighten her hair, once again confined simply by means of a rose satin band holding it back from her forehead, with loose curls falling halfway down her back, and then smoothed down her demure rose and white sprigged muslin gown—an ensemble Max had dubbed her "innocent maiden deserted by her governess and in need of a small loan for coach fare rigout."

Her inspection of her appearance complete, she only had time to press a calming hand to her heaving bosom before the Marquess's loud, imperious knock came on the door. Candie counted slowly to ten before walking with deliberate slowness to the door, calling through it inquiringly, "Who is it, please?"

"Betancourt" was the clipped reply.

"What do you want?" Candie asked, happy to hear how calmly neutral her voice sounded.

"I'm not peddling oranges house to house, if that's what you're worrying about," Betancourt shot back rather testily. "I've come to see you, Miss Murphy, if you'll condescend to opening the door."

"What do you wish to see me about?" she persisted with childlike ingenuity coloring her voice while she held on to her sides to keep from laughing aloud at the thought of keeping the so-sure-of-himself Marquess cooling his elegantly shod heels in the hallway.

"Let me in, Candie, love," he hissed menacingly, "else I'll let the whole building know precisely why and *how* I wish to see you."

He would, too, Candie had no doubt, painfully envisioning the Marquess eloquently or inelegantly—she was not positive on this one point—describing some torrid scene of debauchery his fertile mind was more than capable of producing for her neighbors' benefit. "Just a moment," she called as brightly as she could, beginning another slow count to ten, then hastily pulling open the door as she reached seven and Tony's clear baritone could be heard drawling reminiscently, "Ah, my dearest love, I'll always remember the evening we stole away to my rooms for a few precious moments of privacy. As you rushed headlong

63

into my waiting arms I—well, *hello*, Miss Murphy. How nice of you to ask me to tea."

Pulling the grinning man inside the room, Candie hastily closed the door—but not before Mrs. Clagley, her nearest and nosiest neighbor, had got a good look at her visitor—and went on the attack. "Are you out of your little mind? What do you hope to accomplish by such inexcusable behavior? I have to live in this place for the next few months you know. Max wishes to keep a low profile while we're here and you come knocking down the door spouting ridiculous nonsense designed to having our neighbors complaining to the landlord that we're undesirables. Mrs. Clagley already has it half set in her mind we're running a brothel—I could see it in her eyes, so don't stand there looking like butter wouldn't melt in your mouth—and waltzing in here while my uncle is out only contributes to the appearance of guilt. Oh!" she exploded, the word being uttered in an exasperated growl. "Why can't you just go away and leave us alone? I've had less trouble fending off mad Russians and overzealous bill collectors than I have encountered in attempting to get myself shed of you."

The whole time Candie was speaking—stamping angrily up and down the small room, only stopping once in a while to point an accusing finger in his direction—Tony stood quietly, his weight resting mostly on his left leg, his arms crossed carelessly across his broad chest, and his amused expression nearly inciting Candie to mayhem.

When he was sure she had finished—Candie having flounced to the settee and plopped herself onto it with scant regard for the arrangement of her gown, the furniture's fragile construction, or the fact that she resembled nothing more than an enraged nursery tot who has just been told she could not have another sugarplum—Tony sat down beside her and cradled her clenched hands in his own.

"Let us take this conversation in ascending order of importance," he began smoothly. "First, I am aware you are unchaperoned as I saw Max an hour ago at the Cocoa Tree,

where I imagine he is still, having gained himself an ador-
ing audience of one in Will Merritt, whom I left hanging
on every pearl of wisdom your uncle let dribble from his
mouth, on any subject from Napoleon's errors at Waterloo
to the correct way to judge the quality of small beer.

"That I chose this time to visit brings us to point two.
I'm sorry to have offended Mrs. Clagley's sensibilities, although I rather believe a little excitement will do the old
tabby a world of good, but I am not accustomed to being
reduced to conversing through a closed door, especially
when the person I'm speaking to is setting me up as the
butt of her own warped sense of humor.

"To get down to it without any further silliness or fits of
temper, I am here because we have to decide what I am to
do with you," he ended flatly, realizing as he said the
words that they had not come out sounding at all the way
they should.

Candie made a move to reclaim her hands, but Tony
wasn't ready to relinquish them and, rather than stooping
to a tugging match, Candie allowed him this small victory,
even if his warm touch was doing strange things to her
insides.

"*Do* with me?" she countered, until that moment not
considering any problem but her own. The Marquess, as
she saw it, had picked Max and herself up on a whim, and
he could just as easily put them back down once his curiosity was satisfied. It was Candie who would feel the void his
disappearance would leave in her life while he had a world
of friends — not to mention a plethora of willing females —
about him so that her disappearance would hardly be noticed.

"Yes, pet, *do* with you," he averred, giving a small,
rueful smile. "You and your Uncle Max. What began as a
casual acquaintance has, thanks to m'sister's matchmaking
proclivities and a certain, er, *wager* I entered into with
your uncle, mushroomed, I fear, into a ticklish situation for
us all."

"Have you been drinking?" Candie asked, peering intently into his dark eyes.

Tony laughed deprecatingly. "Sounds that way, don't it? But, no, I'm perfectly sober—not thinking too clearly perhaps, but sober. It's simple, really, if you'll but consider the thing a moment.

"Patsy, that adorable air-head, has taken quite a shine to you and Max and wishes to introduce you about in the winter-thin ranks of society. Before you become too flattered, however, I might point out that Patsy has been bringing home stray dogs, lame pigeons, and a steady stream of wretched, downtrodden souls for as long as I can remember. Lord, you should have seen her late husband! But that's another story. Is it any wonder then that she took one look at you and your ramshackle uncle and immediately decided to take you in hand while you're still young and pretty enough to snag a suitable husband?"

"But I don't *want* a husband," Candie broke in protestingly.

Tony dismissed this argument with a wave of his hand before gathering Candie's fingers once again in his firm grip. "I doubt your wishes are paramount in Patsy's plans. Not only does your beauty challenge her—she sees herself as pulling off a minor coup when you succeed in breaking a half dozen or so hearts—but I fear she is harboring a notion or two concerning a possible match between us. My sister is an incurable romantic, you know."

Again Candie tugged at her bonds and again she failed to gain her freedom. "But that's absurd. A Marquess can't marry a bas—, a nobody like me. I have no background, no dowry. Besides, " she added brightly, as if her information proved her point beyond any glimmering of doubt, "I'm a criminal, a petty conniver. Why, I could be clapped up in Newgate tomorrow. I'm the least suitable bride this side of the moon."

Tony raised one expressive eyebrow. "You want to run that one past Patsy?" he asked facetiously. "Somehow, I don't see her crying off just because of your rather checkered past. Oh no," he said, shaking his head, "you would simply be handing her another cause. First she'd turn your toes back onto the straight and narrow, and *then* she'd throw you at my head."

"Well, she can't launch me into society if I refuse to hoist anchor and set sail," Candie declared after a short pause during which she roundly cursed do-gooders in general and matchmaking sisters in particular, even though she did like Patsy prodigiously. "Max and I will simply decline any invitations. She'll take the hint eventually. After all, even if she is a Betancourt, she's bound to have *some* sense."

At last Candie was given back her hands as Tony rose to pace the room a half dozen times before deciding to make a clean breast of his wager with Max. He described the incident with the workmen and his subsequent obligation to lend his countenance to Patsy's scheme for at least the next fortnight.

He did not dwell on Max's reasons for wishing to see his niece out in society, nor did he see any point in divulging the side stakes for the wager—two weeks of unhampered pursuit of Candie's virtue—especially since he was temporarily, at least, on the losing side.

Since Max had never questioned Candie's decision to remain a spinster, she did not suspect her uncle of anything more than using Lady Montague's establishment as a birthing chamber for yet another of his money-making schemes. That he would be using the unsuspecting Patsy in his pursuit of wealthy, gullible gentlemen eager to be relieved of a portion of their cumbersome fortunes by way of some bogus get-rich-quick scheme designed around, to recall one of Max's earlier successful brainstorms, a surefire way to turn coal into gold, did not set well with her.

But that was family business, not something she would even think of discussing with an outsider like the

Marquess. She'd confront Max when he returned to Half Moon Street, pointing out the cruelty of exposing an innocent like Lady Montague to possible embarrassment or censure, and the two of them would hammer it out between them. Candie was not angered by the realization that her uncle planned to use her in his scheme; in fact, a part of her was disappointed to think about the fun they would miss if Max couldn't find a way to execute his plan without unduly involving Coniston or his sister.

Her bout of concentrated thought resulting in conclusions she found bearable if not entirely comfortable, Candie raised her eyes to look at Tony, who was once again pacing the carpet, still obviously agitated.

"So you lost a wager to Max," she said matter-of-factly. "You will learn, if you spend much more time in his company, that Max only bets on sure things. Actually, I can't remember the last time that jolly conniver lost a wager. No matter. Two weeks shall pass quickly enough, I'm sure, and then we'll be out of your life."

Tony had no great love for the thought of propping up his sister's drawing-room walls while Will Merritt and every other buck made asses of themselves over the beauteous Miss Murphy, no more than he could envision himself engaging in the tame courting expected when dealing with an innocent maiden when he was sure Candie would laugh in his face while he ran about fetching her lemonade and retrieving her misplaced shawl. And he certainly didn't plan to allow Candie to walk out of his life with nothing settled between them.

No, Tony's object had not altered by so much as a hair since first he clapped eyes on Miss Murphy—he intended to bed her as soon as possible. That he had amended this plan to include the possibility of setting her up as his permanent mistress in some discreet little house on the fringes of Mayfair (with Max nowhere in sight) did not overly concern him. He was getting too old to be forever climbing down drainpipes and dodging jealous husbands.

Tony's plan—and he had banked all his hopes on it—centered around getting Max to wager with him again. He didn't care a fig how much blunt Max named as forfeit (as he didn't envision losing again), while his prize would once again be that dreamed-of two weeks of unimpeded pursuit of Miss Murphy's delectable body.

He'd have to stick close to her once she was presented, just to keep the field clear of any Romeo intent on staking a claim to her affections, though it would tax him greatly to watch her putting on ladylike airs when he knew she was no more than an uncommonly pretty shell covering a larcenous soul.

Now that he had put Candie in the picture, so to speak, he felt his former confidence returning, and along with it the firm conviction that Candie was not indifferent to him. Looking at her sitting on the settee with the sun behind her, lighting her white-blonde hair like a halo, he had a momentary twinge as he thought of his plans for her, but although he had indulged himself in a moment or two of wishful thinking earlier in their acquaintance, he no longer harbored the slightest doubt as to Candie's morals—or the lack of them.

She wasn't a paradox, a mixture of cool worldliness housed inside an unworldly, untouched body. That was wishful thinking—although why he would want his mistress to be an innocent was a contradiction he chose not to explore. She was a thief, an intelligent thief, perhaps, but a thief just the same, and it was beyond the realm of possibility that she had lived almost two decades without once taking advantage of her natural attributes in order to reline her empty pockets.

Max put on a fine act—his concerned, loving-uncle role was really quite credible—but, all things considered, it was damned near impossible to swallow. Max was an opportunist, a user, and there was no way he could convince Tony he had been able to withstand the temptation to exploit such a sure money-maker as Candie's delectable body.

The pair had been silent for more than five minutes, both lost in their own thoughts, when Tony belatedly shook his head clear of such unpleasant conjectures and prepared to take his leave.

Candie rose to walk him to the door, apologizing for not serving him any refreshments, and extended a hand in farewell.

Tony looked down at her hand, then up into her seemingly guileless sherry eyes. A promise was a promise, he reminded himself, and he was a man of honor. Two weeks he had agreed to, and two weeks it would be.

Starting five minutes from now!

His hands reaching out to capture her shoulders in a loose embrace, Tony slowly lowered his head to press his lips gently against Candie's soft mouth. Her slight gasp of surprise was followed by a short release of breath, warm, perfumed air Tony drew into his own mouth as he moved to deepen the kiss.

But at the touch of his tongue on the moist inner edge of her bottom lip, Candie, who had been in the act of swaying toward Tony's hard body, drew back sharply, abruptly breaking the contact before taking three quick steps backward and out of the invisible danger zone she had so lately inhabited.

The girl who had glibly talked her way out of more tight spots than a generation of field mice evading a servant maid's lethal broom then found her voice but mislaid her glib tongue, stammering, "Wh-what did you d-do *that* for?"

"That's to seal our truce, my sweetness. You'll do your best to keep Max in line and Patsy happy, and I'll forget my duty to report you and your uncle to the authorities for fraud, wrongful impersonation, and general mischief for the coming fortnight."

"And at the end of that fortnight?" Candie asked, hating her voice for its tendency to quaver. "When your debt to Max is paid in full? What then?"

The Marquess of Coniston was a real treat to behold when he smiled in genuine amusement. His mouth would split into an unabashed grin, showing off his flawless teeth, while his smooth, lean cheeks creased to display long, dimplelike creases, and his dark eyes danced and sparkled and crinkled engagingly at the corners. Just such a heart-stirring sight appeared at Candie's latest question, and while part of her fairly melted under the beauty of the smile, another, saner part of her wished nothing more than to dive into her bed and pull the covers up over her head.

"Why then, my dear, apprehensive gamester," he then drawled maddeningly, "it will be my pleasure to initiate *my* plans concerning your future. It's only fitting, you know, seeing as how Patsy and Max will have had their turn."

"And I'm to have no say in any of this?" Candie asked, her red-brown eyes narrowing dangerously.

Tony reached out his index finger and delivered a playful tap to the side of her nose. "Nary a word," he informed her jauntily, although this time his smile did not quite reach his eyes. Opening the door, he turned, bowed, and stepped over the threshold before glancing back at Candie to see if she was still standing statuelike, her cheeks flushed with indignation.

But to his chagrin, Candie was smiling from her full pink mouth all the way up to her amusement-filled eyes.

"Candie?" he questioned involuntarily, disliking his sudden feeling of being put slightly off balance.

"Good day to you, my lord," was all she replied, already in the act of shutting the door, before adding impetuously, "And it's looking forward I am to hearing all about your plans for me. It's been a long time since I've sparred with anyone even remotely up to my weight. I so dearly love a challenge, don't you know. *Almost* as much as I delight in watching arrogant know-it-all's like you eat crow!"

The door closed in his face before he could think up a fitting retort, leaving Tony to walk away with the infuriating (and perhaps just a tad *unsettling)* sound of Candie's confident laughter ringing in his ears.

As he emerged out onto the flagway, his shoulders stiffened as mentally he reclassified his pending pursuit of Candie's questionable virtue, filing it instead under the heading "Murphy Assault Plan," not being so obtuse as to still believe he had but to dangle a bauble or two under Candie's nose to have her falling into his arms, not after she had just hurled a figurative gauntlet at his feet.

Every time he saw her he wanted her more, and her easy reading of and immediate opposition to his intentions had intensified rather than lessened his desire. Not only would she decorate his bed, she would delight his senses. For no ignorant opera dancer or dull-as-ditch-water jaded society matron was Miss Candice Murphy. Even their arguments—and it seemed they argued every time they met—excited him. Soon there was to be a mighty battle, of the wits as well as the senses, and when she surrendered (as he knew she would), they would come together as equals, both giving and taking freely as was their right.

Tony's muscles tightened as he savored an intoxicating vision of Candie's eventual fate. Maybe he'd buy her a modest retreat in the country as well as the town house. And if he promises to behave himself, he mused, feeling magnanimous, I may just let Max visit her from time to time.

Candie, watching from her vantage point behind the lace curtains, followed Tony's progress down Half Moon Street, her smile slowly fading as she realized that no matter who technically emerged the victor in their little battle of wills, she would inevitably end up the loser.

If she succumbed to Tony's bound-to-be nearly irresistible campaign of seduction, she would not only have broken her well-thought-out and heretofore heartfelt vow to remain chaste, but she would have opened the door to the heartbreak that awaited her once he tired of her charms.

But if she bested him, if she resisted his blandishments and succeeded in forcing him to admit defeat, she would lose again. For then he would take his exit from her life, again leaving her brokenhearted. *If I let him seduce me,* she told herself with a slightly hysterical giggle, *at least I'll have my memories to keep my broken heart company.*

Allowing the curtains to drop back into place, she resolutely turned away from the window and Coniston's departing form, reminding herself of the parting shot she had fired—her brave announcement that she looked forward to the excitement of matching wits with him.

It was true that Candie had inherited Max's love of playing the game, going along with his schemes more for the mental exercise and the thrill of outfoxing her opponent than any thought of material gain, but soon she would be playing for the largest stakes of her career—herself.

And she would go it alone, without enlisting her uncle's aid and thus giving herself an unfair advantage. Let Max weave his webs around targets gleaned from the potential victims he would meet at Lady Montague's. She'd let him play this hand alone, while she pretended to go along with his ridiculous trumped-up story about wanting his niece to enter society. She had no time to play wealthy investor to one of her uncle's captive audiences of greedy fools, no time to waste in endless hours of carefully penning genuine looking shares of stock in The Great Chinese Fireworks Consortium (written entirely in Chinese, of course) to be sold at the unheard of low price of fifty pounds a share.

No, outmaneuvering Tony as he sought to undermine her defenses and launching a counterattack meant to discourage him once and for all would give her more than enough to occupy her every waking hour.

She sank to her knees beside the ornate cradle, idly rocking it back and forth as she reviewed her knowledge of Tony Betancourt, searching for some chink in his armor or self-confidence that would give her the advantage she needed.

For the first time in her career, such conjuring did not afford her the slightest bit of pleasure.

Chapter Six

CANDIE'S NOTE to Lady Montague informing her that, due to unforeseen circumstances, she and her uncle would have to decline her kind invitation to participate in her ladyship's card party, was met with a scribbled response hand-delivered by Patsy's second underfootman, demanding Candie present herself in Portman Square immediately.

As Candie was not adverse to spending the morning in Lady Montague's company, and with precious little to do on Half Moon Street, she bade the underfootman wait while she grabbed her pelisse and bonnet, begging the man's company for the brisk walk up Park Lane.

Once seated in the small, elaborately decorated sitting room Patsy favored for intimate chats, Candie was amply entertained casting her gaze about the place, noting how Patsy's flighty personality was so firmly stamped on this room filled with light and color and ridiculously ornate feminine fripperies while the rest of the mansion, or at least as much of it as she had seen on her first visit, leaned more toward the dark, and even the funereal.

"This room is exceptionally vulgar, isn't it?" Patsy asked breezily, entering the room, her stylishly draped negligee floating about her and making her look like a small yacht in full sail. "But it does suit me, don't you think?"

"What I think, my lady," Candie replied, her sherry eyes twinkling, "is that I would give a great deal to have met your husband. You must have been as alike as chalk and cheese."

"Harry?" Patsy said questioningly, screwing up her perfectly shaped nose. She looked about the room, filled floor to ceiling with treasures her late husband would have termed garbage, and allowed her features to re-form into an impish grin. "Oh, Harry would have had a rare fit if he could have seen his sanctuary turned out in such lamentably poor taste. He ran more to horrid paintings of dead game—you know the sort, the kind where the poor little animals lie limply at some brave huntsman's feet, blood running from their sides—and furnishings whose styles and colors I found to be most depressing indeed. How astute of you, Candie, to notice."

After summoning a servant and issuing orders for tea and cakes to be served immediately (and then exploding her image of grande dame by smiling widely and saying "Please, Haswick"), Lady Montague sat herself down beside Candie and demanded to know why the Murphys had refused her invitation.

"Uncle Max has, er, been called away unexpectedly on business, I'm afraid," Candie told her hostess, finding herself averting her gaze as she found herself unable to lie directly into the woman's guileless blue eyes.

Those blue eyes widened perceptively. "But then you're *all alone* in the city! How can you stay alone on Half Moon Street? How long will he be gone?"

"Truth to tell, I don't know when Max will be back, as

76

his plans were rather fluid. But don't concern yourself, my lady. *Uncail* is like the proverbial bad penny and will show up again."

"But that's perfectly dreadful!" her ladyship exclaimed, leaving Candice to wonder whether her ladyship was referring to Max's absence or his inevitable return. "And what are you supposed to do in the meantime? A young girl alone in London? I vow, I cannot believe your uncle to be so blind to his responsibility."

Candie could tell that Lady Montague was genuinely concerned and tried to ease her mind. "I imagine you must see ours as a rather raffish way of living, but I assure you I am perfectly capable of fending for myself for the sennight or so that Max will be gone. After all, it's not like it's the first time."

Patsy clutched her hands to her generous bosom, the only one of Lady Montague's many possessions Candie could truly say she coveted for her own, and shook her head so violently her ebony curls danced about her head. "Please, I beg you not to tell me any more, dearest Candie, for I do not think I could bear it." Then, suddenly seeming to hit on a solution that would keep her from believing her new friend would be murdered in her bed before the week was out, Lady Montague's dazzling smile banished the last traces of anxiety from her lovely face. "I have it!" she fairly shrieked, hugging the dumbstruck Candie to her breast. "You shall move in here with me until your uncle returns. Oh, Candie, I vow it will be famous. We'll be as merry as grigs, shopping, and entertaining, and staying up to the wee hours talking in my bedchamber."

Candie sat rigid in Patsy's embrace, a look of shock on her face, her unblinking eyes staring into the middle distance as Patsy went on to wax poetic over the glorious time they would have. Stay with Lady Montague in Portman Square? Stay with Tony's own sister when she knew what she knew, both of Tony's disenchantment with her association with his sister and of Max's plans to use the mansion

77

in Portman Square for leads on his search for pigeons ripe for the plucking? Stay with dear, scatter-witted Patsy, who was trying her best to marry Candie off?

Then a small smile appeared on Candie's face. Stay with Patsy, where not even Tony Betancourt would dare accost her with either his threats or his attempts at seduction? Stay in Portman Square, where her very presence would have that same Tony Betancourt growling and gnashing his teeth, totally powerless as he watched Candie work her wiles on Will Merritt and all the other eligible young gentlemen Patsy planned to parade by her?

Fighting back any lingering feelings that she was, thanks to Max, being handed about like a sack of meal— being picked up by her uncle, Tony, and Patsy and placed down in localities of their choosing—Candie concentrated on the nasty but still quite pleasing feeling of having bested Tony once again. Getting herself tucked up smartly in his sister's motherly embrace would go a long way in getting some of her own back from the smug Marquess of Coniston.

Disengaging herself from Patsy's embrace, Candie smiled her sweetest, most self-effacing smile and, lowering her eyes shyly, accepted Lady Montague's kind invitation. The demonstrative Patsy, thrilled all the way down to her petite painted toes that she would have a whole week of Candie's pleasant company, swept the girl into yet another perfumed embrace, which Candie returned with real feeling, for it was impossible not to like Tony's sister.

The older woman sat back, still not releasing Candie's hands, and pouted prettily. "Now that we are to be bosom chums, Candie, I must insist that you call me Patsy. I declare, it's been an age since I've felt like I had a real female friend."

"Patsy it is," Candie agreed, feeling herself well and truly caught up in Lady Montague's excitement.

Squirming around in her seat in order to face Candie, Patsy began rhapsodizing on the many adventures they would have once Candie was installed in Portman Square, which would be directly after luncheon if the young widow had anything to say on the matter. "We'll go through your wardrobe at once, just so we are sure you won't need any additions. Oh, I do so hope you do, as I just adore shopping. Why, Harry used to say—"

"Cleopatra!" a loud, strident female voice penetrated to every nook and cranny in the room and, Candie imagined, set the fragile figurines to trembling. "Look at you!" the voice went on. "Nearly noon and still dressed in that ridiculous negligee. Thirty years old and still without a single lick of sense. What my Harry ever saw in such a sad clunch as you escapes me. That poor boy, tied to a brainless chit half his age and then hurried into his grave by her hey-go-mad ways. Why, I—"

Candie could barely restrain herself from flinching, Patsy's grip on her fingers pained her so, and she looked past her friend's shoulder to locate the author of this nasty speech. What she saw made her bite down hard on her bottom lip to keep from disgracing herself by breaking into vulgar guffaws. For there, in all her ridiculously overdone mourning draperies, stood Miss Ivy Dillingham, one of the London pigeons Max had plucked to a fare-thee-well not eighteen months earlier as he passed himself off as a lottery king selling chances in a half dozen mines in South America. Knowing Miss Dillingham would never recognize her as Juan Montoya, the bogus Lord Fairchild's South American partner, kept her from feeling any fear of discovery and free to sit back to discover just what the formidable but oh so obtuse woman was doing running tame in Patsy's sitting room.

"Ivy!" Patsy had exclaimed hastily, cutting off the older woman's attack as she at last let go of Candie's hands and strove to rearrange herself in some semblance of dignity. "How, um, unexpected, yes, unexpected*ly, nice,* yes, *nice* to see you," she stumbled, flushing. "No! I mean, not that I didn't *expect* it to be nice to see you. I mean, I didn't

79

mean to see you—*no!* That's not what I meant. I mean to say—"

"Oh, do shut up, Cleopatra," Miss Dillingham cut in just as Patsy was in danger of strangling on her twisted tongue. The very short, very round woman walked heavily across the room to seat herself in a chair that, if chairs could speak, would have set up an instant howl of pain. "Who is this, Cleopatra? Didn't Harry manage to teach you anything? Introduce us, you widget."

"Murphy, you say?" Miss Dillingham mused once Patsy had stuttered her way through the formalities, clearly intimidated by the woman she had just identified to Candie as being her late husband's sister. "I don't believe I know any Murphys. Irish, ain't it? I do know some O'Hares," she said, her voice trailing off.

It was too good to resist. If Miss Dillingham hadn't been such a thoroughly disagreeable person she never would have done it, but the woman had upset Patsy—and not for the first time, Candie wagered—and the imp of mischief that was just then sitting on her shoulder nudged her into speech. "Would that be the sheep-stealing O'Hares, the barn-burning O'Hares, or the well-poisoning O'Hares, Miss Dillingham?" she trilled, her sherry eyes widening innocently.

It was some moments before Patsy, who had been sipping some restorative tea at the time, could be rescued from her fit of coughing, time in which Miss Dillingham gathered the cloak of injured respectability about herself and prepared to snuff young Miss Murphy's insolence. "Where is your *dame de compagnie,* Miss Murphy?" she asked in quelling (and atrocious) accents. "I saw no maid sitting in the foyer below. Cleopatra, don't tell me you have taken to entertaining young females of questionable reputation. Even as a, perish the thought, high-flying young widow, it is not *comme il faut* to so flaunt the conventions."

Oh, thought Patsy as she felt herself flushing like a schoolgirl caught in a fib, no one was ever more provoking than Ivy. It was one thing to take after *her,* Lord knew she was used to it, but it was quite another for the old harridan to attack a guest in this house. Rousing herself to the mild show of indignation that was as high as her rarely used temper ever climbed, Patsy was struck by a sudden inspiration. "Miss Murphy's abigail was discharged for—for theft. It was very distressing, really, finding the girl sneaking out of the house in the dead of night, Candie's pearl necklace tied up in a handkerchief. But, as she is my houseguest for this week or more we thought it preferable for us to share my Alice until her uncle, Mr. Maximilien P. Murphy, returns to the city and can interview a suitable replacement." Sighing deeply in satisfaction over her brilliance, Patsy then sank back against the settee and smiled. "You see, Ivy, it is all most unexceptionable."

"Indeed," Miss Dillingham sniffed, still bristling over Candie's little joke at her expense. Look at the girl, she thought, running her small black eyes up and down Candie's figure, sitting there looking for all the world like some second-rate artist's idea of an angel. Surely that white hair was nothing more than a botched dye job. She was a nobody, and an Irish nobody at that. Just the sort of creature Cleopatra would take to.

Although she didn't speak any of her thoughts aloud, Candie knew what the old biddy was thinking. Harry's sister, huh, she mused consideringly. Older sister, I'll wager, and a spinster at that. What would Max have said? Oh, yes. It would seem her intended husband's mother died an old maid. Lucky woman, Candie thought—and lucky unborn husband. She was glad Max had fleeced her so royally. How Patsy stood having the woman for a sister-in-law was beyond Candie's comprehension. "Indeed," she said now, "I am greatly indebted to Lady Montague for her kindness in taking me in while my uncle is away. But, of course, being related to Patsy, even if yours is not a blood relation and even if the reason for associating with each other is now enjoying his eternal reward, you don't have to be reminded of the great privilege it is to be an *invited* guest in this house."

It would have been nice to think that Candie's barely veiled pointing out of Miss Dillingham's lack of invitation, combined with Patsy's very obvious distress at her presence, would serve to discommode the woman to the point where she would take her leave. Alas, this was not to be the case. Interminable minutes were to pass, a trying time filled entirely by Miss Dillingham's homilies on manners, deportment, the general flightiness of the younger generation, and the sad state of affairs a house must face when its guiding force (in this case, one Harry Dillingham, the late Lord Montague) was no longer in charge, before, having at last shot her bolt, Ivy departed in a wave of cloying scent.

"Phew!" Candie commented, waving her hand in front of her nose once she and Patsy were alone. "Besides being the most totally disagreeable female it has ever been my misfortune to encounter outside the headmistress of my last boarding school, that woman wears enough perfume to stun an ox at twenty paces. Patsy, however do you bear it—not to mention *why* do you bear it?"

Patsy pulled a pained expression, meant to look long-suffering but serving only to make her resemble a scolded child. "She's Harry's only sister, you understand, and I feel I should at least keep a good front on things. Ivy won't admit it, but Harry was happy with me for the five years we were together, and I owe the poor man something, don't I?"

"Was Harry much like her?" Candie asked, trying with all her might to picture Patsy married to such a person.

"Good Lord, no," Patsy laughed, preening a bit. "Harry was a bit odd—odd enough to marry me when everyone said I should either retire to the country to raise dogs or go on the stage, as no one would ever marry such a brainless widget as me no matter if I had both face and fortune as inducement—but we rubbed along fairly well until he died. What a sad business that was, Candie. Snuffed like a candle, the poor man, and we had been dancing all the night long at Lady Sefton's before he just rolled back his eyes—right there on the dance floor in the middle of a lovely quadrille—and dropped like a stone. I do believe Lady Sefton holds the grudge to this day. It certainly put the period to her ball, let me tell you."

Holding back a smile, an exercise that took her greatest efforts, Candie remarked as innocently as she could, "Well, I do see where Harry's unexpected demise might have put a minor crimp in her guests' enjoyment of the festivities."

"Oh, yes," Patsy said artlessly. "I understand she was left with a veritable mountain of melting Gunther Ices when everyone went home without so much as going down to supper. As if filling their bellies would be some sort of insult to poor Harry, who would have been appalled at the waste of such good food. Ices were his particular favorite, you understand."

Noting that, as if to belie Patsy's superficial-sounding comments, the woman's lower lip was exhibiting a lamentable tendency to quiver, Candie quickly changed the subject. "Don't you think, seeing as how you do not seem to deal very well together, it would perhaps be best if you saw less of Miss Dillingham?"

"*I* don't see her at all, Candie," Patsy contradicted. "*She* sees me. I do believe she feels she must keep me in line as a service to Harry. At times I actually pity her, for Harry was her life you know, but I must admit I sometimes find Ivy to be excessively disagreeable." Lady Montague was silent for a moment, then smiled impishly. "Actually, I *always* find her to be excessively disagreeable!"

Candie took up her cue. "I thought I would disgrace myself entirely and burst out laughing when she was lecturing us on proper behavior. It put me in mind, as I said before, of my last stint at boarding school and Miss Hardcastle's incessant recitation of Mr. Matthew Towle's book for children. The man was a dancing master who imagined himself the arbiter of juvenile behavior. I do believe I can still recite it word for word."

At Patsy's pleading, Candie rose and walked to the center of the room, where she stood in a demure pose, eyes cast down, and her hands clasped behind her back. "'When you receive orders to go into the room where your parents are,'" she began in a singsong voice, "'bow, stand still till such time they bid you sit down or inform you what is their pleasure with you—'"

"Oh, dear, yes," Patsy broke in, rolling her eyes. "In my case, the 'pleasure' was usually a stern lecture for something I had done. Please, Candie, go on. I think it's famous!"

Candie, happy to see her new friend smiling once again, complied. "'Sit still, upright, and silent,'" she intoned awfully. "'Look not at anyone that is in the room, so as not to stare or ogle at them. Play not with anything about you, viz., buttons, handkerchief, and the like. Put not your fingers in your mouth, bite not your nails, make no faces—' Patsy," Candie broke off, laughing. "Stop making faces!"

Patsy, who had been busily acting out all of the actions Candie had so far recited, only giggled and crossed her eyes.

"To continue," Candie pushed on, her voice taking on the arctic monotone of Miss Hardcastle, "'Make no noise with your feet, put not your hands in your pockets. Turn your toes out, lay not one leg over the other.'"

Unbeknownst to either of the young ladies now convulsed with mirth, Tony Betancourt, paying a morning visit on his only sister, had heard their laughter and was even now standing at the entrance to the room, taking in the scene unfolding in front of him. Urchin, he thought in amusement, watching Candie as she posed and postured, giving a splendid imitation of every headmistress and headmaster ever born, and surprised himself by finding himself to be quite proud of her performance.

"'If you cannot avoid sneezing—'"

Patsy obligingly sneezed into her handkerchief.

"'Or coughing—'"

Patsy's cough was, Tony realized, grinning, their father's loud bark to the life.

Favoring Patsy with her sternest headmistress look, Candie intoned crushingly, "'Turn aside and make as *little* noise in doing so as you possibly can. It is very *vulgar* in anyone to make a noise in coughing and sneezing—'"

"And nearly impossible not to," Patsy pointed out before once again demonstrating both vulgar indulgences.

"'You should have a special care not to make any kind of faces, that is grinning, winking, or putting out your tongue, and the like,'" Candie ended, her face a solemn, forbidding mask, "*'for that will make you despised!'*"

Patsy clapped her hands in delight. "Oh yes, I always abhorred that part. I once held back a sneeze for so long that my eyes watered and Papa refused to punish me because I looked so penitent, when I really was just trying not to have him despise me. How I worried that they would not love me." She then sighed reminiscently.

This admission took Tony by surprise, as he would have sworn Patsy never worried a lick about anything. "Papa fairly doted on you, puss," he said, entering the room and giving his sister a kiss on the cheek. "Why else do you think I put that frog in your bed if it wasn't out of jealousy?"

Candie stood back and enjoyed the sight of brother and sister smiling over shared memories. Really, she mused consideringly, if he weren't so dreadfully disconcerting to her emotions, Tony would be her choice for the brother she'd never had. Patsy was a lucky woman.

When Patsy at last released him, Coniston turned to greet Candie with genuine friendliness, happy to see her positive effect on his sister, but his smile hardened into a grimace as Patsy gushed out the news that Miss Murphy was to be her houseguest while Mr. Murphy was away on business. "Patsy, love," he said from between clenched teeth, "I saw your maid in the hallway, and she said to remind you of that appointment with your modiste this afternoon. You look fetching as you are, but I believe your maid may have laid out a more suitable ensemble for Bond Street."

"Oh, lud!" Patsy exclaimed, gathering her draperies about her as she jumped to her feet. "I have a mind like a sieve, don't I? Well," she flustered, realizing she was leaving Candie unchaperoned, but then dismissing any fears as ludicrous, as it was, after all, only Tony, "I'll be just as quick as I can. You two amuse yourselves for a moment, and then we'll all have a nice luncheon before my appointment."

Once she had reached the relative safety of the hallway, Patsy shivered at the look she had seen in Tony's dark eyes. She had, somewhere in her flighty brain, realized that Tony might not like her plans for Candie above half, but it had not occurred to her that he would outwardly oppose her scheme. Now, closing her eyes and giving her head a little shake, she was not so sure. Tony had long since graduated from frogs in her bed when it came to showing his displeasure for any of her actions.

The chill that pervaded the room once Patsy had dropped her verbal bomb had made Candie retreat to her former seat on the settee in an attempt to cushion the force of Tony's inevitable icy blast of temper. She didn't have long to wait.

"All right, madam," he said, attacking the moment he was sure Patsy was out of earshot. "I doubt it will improve with keeping. Tell me, what maggot has Max taken into his head now?"

Momentarily nonplussed that Tony had dismissed his obvious disenchantment with Patsy's plans in order to take umbrage with her uncle, Candie could only stall for time. "Why do you ask that?"

Tony arranged his handsome face in a knowing sneer. "Because I'm beginning to know how that larcenous leprechaun thinks, that's why. Come clean, Candie, what rig is he running now? And why aren't you with him—although I'm glad to see the man's finally getting some sense into his head, even if that does mean he's deserted you."

"I don't know where he is," Candie responded with more heat than she would have liked.

"Tell me another one," Betancourt said contemptuously.

"Salvation seize your soul," Candie retorted in Max's best brogue, "and why should I be lying to you?"

Tony allowed himself a small smile. "Force of habit?" he offered drily.

Her sense of humor touched, Candie gave in and told him what she knew, which wasn't much. Max, clad in his Budge-Budge costume and carrying a small valise, had departed early that morning, saying he could be reached at the Pulteney if Candie needed him.

"Budge-Budge!" Coniston spat contemptuously. "I should have known he was up to something when he didn't meet me this morning. After failing to run him to ground on Half Moon Street, I gambled on finding him here running some rig on m'sister."

"Instead, you found me here running some rig on your sister?" Candie prompted with infuriating insight.

"Indeed," he concurred coldly. "However, I'll have to deal with you later. Right now I'm off to put a spoke in Max's wheel before he lands us all in Newgate."

"So it's off to the Pulteney you are, with your fingers in your mouth?" Candie spat contemptuously, causing Lord Coniston to halt in his tracks and whirl about to face her.

"And just what do you mean by that earthy Irish proverb?"

"It means you're off on a fool's errand, and no mistake," Candie told him smugly, looking more relaxed than she had since he first entered the room.

Tony bristled a moment, but then his ego reasserted itself. "I think not, madam. For the day has not dawned that I shall be made a fool of."

"Googeen," Candie muttered under her breath, employing the Irish term for "simpleminded" as she watched Tony stride out the door.

"Has Tony gone, then?" Patsy asked when she returned to the room some minutes later.

"That he has," Candie said sweetly, smiling at her friend. "And there's many a dry eye after him."

Chapter Seven

THE PULTENEY HOTEL, with its impressive stone pillars and modern bow windows, looked out across Picadilly on the deer and cattle that browsed near the white-stuccoed Ranger's Lodge in Green Park and the red-bricked facade of Buckingham House, the whole framed by the Abbey towers and the soft Surrey hills. It was one of the most exclusive and most expensive hotels in the city, and as Lord Coniston hurriedly vaulted up the wide steps and passed into the vast lobby, he was not surprised to see the place stiff with the rich, the titled, and the mighty.

That Maximilien would dare to run another Budge-Budge rig did not surprise Tony in the slightest. But the idea of using the Pulteney as his base of operations was a move the Marquess deemed to be foolhardy in the extreme. Can't say the man lacks audacity, Tony thought as he searched out "his highness's" private suite.

Tony knocked imperiously on the heavily paneled door,

which opened under the force of his clenched fist, and strode into the room prepared to do battle.

"I cannot thank you enough for your offer to mention me to his royal highness, your excellency," Sir George Ringley, a very small cog in the ministry office, was saying with earnest subservience as he bowed in half from the waist.

"'Tis nothing," the Maharajah of Budge-Budge, sitting cross-legged in regal splendor amid a dozen silken cushions, replied in a heavily accented singsong voice. Coniston could not fail to notice the matched set of chased silver goblets resting at Max's feet, obviously put there by Sir George in an overt act of bribery. A quick look about the sitting room revealed the place to be cluttered with similar "welcoming gifts," ranging from silver tea sets to framed oil paintings.

Greed has many faces, Tony mused, shaking his head at the folly of his fellow man, and Max has turned taking advantage of that greed into an art form. "We meet again, your highness," he said now, causing Sir George to straighten hurriedly and turn to see who else had come to curry favor from the visiting Maharajah.

"Coniston!" Sir George smiled smugly, thinking he had scored a minor coup in courting Budge-Budge if the man hobnobbed with the likes of the Marquess.

"Ringley," Tony returned lazily, running his gaze up and down the other man before saying dismissingly, "You were, I earnestly hope, on your way out?"

Once Sir George had bowed and scraped his way ungracefully from the suite, Tony closed the door with a meaningful slam and turned to attack. "The Devil take your bladder, Max," he ejaculated sharply. "We'll all end in the suds yet, no thanks to you!"

Max ignored this outburst, lifting one of the silver goblets to inspect it, saying, "Nice, don't you think? I tried to knock another shilling or two out of him, but it's miserly he is, and 'tisn't today or yesterday it happened to him."

Tony distractedly ran a hand through his carefully arranged dark locks and stormed over to snatch up a newspaper that was lying on a side table. "Where is it, Max? Out with it! I know it's in here somewhere."

Murphy didn't bother to dissemble. "Page six, lad," he answered, arranging his pillows about him so that he resembled nothing more than a plump spider sitting in his web awaiting prey.

Nearly tearing the pages in his haste, Coniston soon located the black-edged notice announcing the Maharajah of Budge-Budge's arrival in the city as well as his willingness to greet journalists and government dignitaries at the Pulteney Hotel for the period of three days before his audience with his royal highness. "This is nothing more than an advertisement for bribes and you know it," Tony accused, stabbing a finger at the notice.

"It wasn't an invitation to tea," Max agreed cordially, leaning back against his cushions and reaching under a bright red one to extract a fat roll of bills. "The geegaws are nice enough, but give me a man who understands the power of hard cash. I've enough here already to take a good-sized flutter on the bangtails. Sit yourself down, Coniston. You're as skittish as a dog around an Irishman's boot."

Tony subsided into a chair, whether on Max's orders or not he didn't know. "You're crazy, do you know that? What if someone takes the time to find you out?"

"Who?" Max snorted. "Which one of the host of English milords who've been traipsing through here greasing my palm do you think to be smart enough to find me out?" He arranged the bank notes like a fan and waved them under his nose. "Ah, Tony, me lad, I'm on the pig's back now, don't you know. Sure beats being a barker for a bow-wow shop. Food's good here too."

"You may be in high fettle now, Max, but your luck's bound to run out soon," Coniston told him repressively.

Max just shook his head. "Time enough to bid the Devil

good morrow when you meet him, I always say. But you never mind that. I hear you've been haunting the house on Half Moon Street. Thinking of breaking our bargain, are you?"

"One visit doesn't constitute a haunting, Max," Tony responded archly, still chafing a bit over his confrontation with Candie. "Besides, I think the whole thing is a moot point now that Candie's moved in with m'sister."

Max's smile was maddeningly cherubic. "Has she now?" he purred. "And what brought this on, I'll be asking?"

Giving the older man a short, pithy account of what he had learned in Portman Square, Tony tried to get back to his original argument. "You may be having a rare good time tweaking noses here at the Pulteney but, burn it man, you're putting Candie smack in harm's way with your antics. Do you mean to land the girl in jail with you?"

Tony's accusation succeeded at last in rousing Max from his nest of silken cushions. "The Devil mend ye, lad, I'll not stand by and listen to sermons from the likes of you. Or was that some other Marquess of Coniston who wished to win two weeks' worth of unhampered seduction time from the girl's own uncle? I release you from that bet, by the by, seeing as how your own sister has taken up the role of dragon in Candie's defense. Always lands on her feet, does my sweet Candice."

Tony propped his elbows on his knees and let his forehead sink into his hands. "Now I know how my Uncle Frederic felt when my father had him locked up in Ringmer for saying Joan of Arc gave him orders to march on London." Lifting his head, he gave sanity one last shot. "Now that Candie's safeguarded from my lascivious pursuit, won't you consider ending this charade? Surely you've got enough stuff here to keep you in Irish whiskey for a while."

The Irishman looked about the suite at his booty, mentally calculating its worth in the nearest pawnshop, and tried to estimate how much more he could hope to garner if he were to stay at the Pulteney for another two days. "Very well, boyo. I'll do it, please God," he then intoned seriously, looking Tony square in the eye to show his sincerity.

"That's the ticket, Max!" Tony applauded enthusiastically. "I knew you'd put Candie's well-being ahead of anything else."

Murphy smiled modestly, knowing as Tony did not that he had agreed to nothing. After all, if he chose to stay at the Pulteney, it would obviously be because God's pleasure had been denied him. It was a classic Irish "out," but it would serve him well enough if Candie didn't get wind of it.

Each of the men satisfied that he had bested the other, the two now settled back for a comfortable chat, as they did truly enjoy each other's company no matter what their differences. In time, Tony touched on his visit to Portman Square, and Ivy Dillingham's name slid into the conversation.

"Dillingham, did you say?" Max questioned, stroking his chin. "Spinster, as I recall, and so short and fat that if you were to meet her on the street you'd sooner jump over her than walk round her?"

Tony gave a bark of laughter. "That's Ivy," he concurred, relishing the vivid mental image Max's words conjured up. "How do you know the lady?"

Believing the details of that meeting to be best left well buried, Max parried, "Oh, around town somewhere. Not my cup o'tea, you know. Wouldn't do to go hat in hand to that gorgon, let me tell you, if you were ever in need of charity. Not that she'd turn you away, mind, but, like my mother used to say, if she had only an egg she'd give you the shell."

"You must tell Patsy that one," Tony chuckled. "She'd greatly appreciate your opinion of her sister-in-law."

Shaking his head, Max intoned soberly, "It's more like a warning I'd give your sister, my boyo. I tell you, the woman is the sort who'd stand at your back while your nose is breaking. No, Lady Montague is no match for that harpy. As her brother, I suggest you keep a sharp eye on her so she doesn't come to harm. Pity her ladyship can't find it in her heart to marry Mr. Kinsey. He'd not stand for any nonsense from Miss Dillingham."

"You noticed that?" Tony asked, clearly impressed with Max's powers of observation concerning the love-struck Kinsey.

"Boyo, I notice everything," Max said, winking. "Why else do you think I'm letting you near my Candie?"

Tony did not understand exactly what Max meant by this last statement, unless it was to mean that the man dismissed him as harmless. Hardly a flattering assessment, the Marquess thought, but if it satisfied Max, who was he to quibble? After a few more minutes of conversation, during which Max readily agreed to Tony's every suggestion concerning vacating the suite at the Pulteney before the day was out, Tony took his leave, holding the door open for the affluent merchant who, like all the others, came bearing gifts.

"Sir, your most obedient," the Marquess intoned, bowing himself out. He too could "play the game."

"There goes a right fine fool of a man, so besotted with my Candie I could lead him to her with a halter of snow," Max whispered under his breath before spreading his hands in welcome to his next victim.

It was almost an hour past midnight when the Marquess of Coniston called again on the mansion in Portman Square, but he was considerate enough not to bother waking Patsy's ancient butler by hammering on the knocker. It was kinder, he told himself, as well as more expedient to climb the drainpipe that so conveniently ran alongside the bedchamber most likely to have been assigned to Candice.

Mister Overnite, thanks to long years of practice, made short work of both the ascent and his subsequent entry through an unlocked window. Dropping lightly to the floor on stockinged feet, he was rewarded by the sight of Candice Murphy sound asleep in the high tester bed sitting in the middle of the room.

She did not plait her hair for the night, he observed, smiling. Seeing that glorious curtain of white-gold spread out over her pillow did more than a little to ease his conscience at his second-story work. After all, it may not have been *his* pillow, but at least his fantasy had come true in part. Lying there, her pink, pouting mouth softened in sleep, Candie was like his dream come to life, and he was hard pressed not to slide into the bed beside her and wake her with his kiss.

He gave himself a mental shake. No, he was getting ahead of himself. He was not here for seduction. All right, then, Mark Antony, he asked himself facetiously, what *are* you here for?

"What are you doing here?"

Tony lifted back his head with a snap as Candie's calmly asked question mirrored his own thoughts. Stepping further into the room, he saw that her huge sherry eyes were alive with mischief, and not a drop of fear, as she lay quite still under the covers.

"I came to tell you I went to the Pulteney and saw Max," he was startled into saying.

"Of course you did," Candie agreed maddeningly, propping up her pillows and sitting back against them for all the world like she was holding court. "And now you can rush hotfoot back to Max and tell him you have been to Portman Square and seen me. My, what a wild social life you English peers do lead."

He was torn between the lingering urge to kiss her and a new, strong desire to throttle her for her sharp tongue. Crossing over to sit on the side of the bed, he stated firmly, "I bearded your uncle in his den at the Pulteney and got his promise to vacate the premises before someone discovers his little charade."

"Promised you, did he?" Candie remarked, amusement

coloring her voice. "And you believed him? *Uncail* tells some shocking rappers you know."

"I don't trust your uncle across the street," Coniston shot back testily. "I just wanted you to know that I did my best. I thought you'd be grateful. After all, he could get you both into serious trouble."

Candie snuggled back comfortably against the pillows. "Don't pick me up till I fall, Coniston," she said, her eyes narrowing just a trifle. "I can take care of myself, thank you very much. And as for my uncle, why, come Judgement Day, Max will run a rig on the Lord."

Tony decided to abandon this line of conversation for another. "We have other business to discuss, Miss Murphy. For one, how did you manage to get yourself dug in here with m'sister?"

"You introduced us, remember?"

"That is something I particularly regret," he retaliated, feeling more than a little frustrated. "I'll say this for you though, madam, you surely know how to make the most of a chance meeting in the Park."

Candie's sherry eyes narrowed to slits. "I'll be polite to a point, Coniston, but not beyond it. I have chosen thus far to overlook the fact that you have broken into my bed-chamber. I have even allowed you to malign my uncle, seeing as how it seems to have become your favorite hobby. But you're beginning to disturb my peace more than a little bit. I need not remind you that all I need do is scream to have this entire household down on you like a shot. How dare you think I'd ever take advantage of Patsy?"

"I've misjudged you?" Tony quipped sarcastically. "Silly me. I should have realized you are a paragon of virtue. It must have been meeting you in the guardhouse that threw me off."

Throwing back the covers so that they enveloped Tony's head, Candie fairly leapt from the bed and dove into her robe. "You're a real piece of work, do you know that?" she accused in a harsh whisper. "All this to-do over your sister falling victim to me when you let that odious Ivy Dillingham flap around here like some vulture who scents fresh blood. If it's protecting Patsy you're so hot to do, why not start by getting her shed of that predator?"

"That vulture is Harry's sister. Patsy feels a responsibility toward her."

"And Patsy is incredibly silly," Candie pointed out without malice. "Kind, endearingly sweet, and impossible to dislike, but a true featherbrained innocent. She should marry Hugh Kinsey and have done with it. *He'd* give the Dillingham short shrift."

Tony shook his head in amazement. "Is there nothing gets round you people? I don't know why Hugh don't just give it up and take an ad in the *Times.*"

Candie stopped her angry pacing and threw the Marquess what was intended to be a quelling look, but if it was intimidation she was after, the result fell far short of the mark. For Mark Antony Betancourt was, even at this ungodly hour of the night and even though she was quite put out with him, still the one man in the world who could turn her limbs to water with a smile. She clutched her robe more tightly about her, for much as she was used to being seen in her nightgown by her uncle, she was suddenly quite aware of her state of near undress. "Please go now," she almost pleaded, causing Tony to lift his head and stare at her in amazement.

"What's wrong, puss?" he asked, rising to walk toward her. "Are you having a belated attack of missishness?"

She glared at him balefully. Wasn't it enough that he could see her discomfiture? Did he have to comment on it? "You're no gentleman," she said astringently.

"Shall I reply with the obvious?" crooned Tony, still advancing on her. "It's monstrous inconvenient for a seduction here at Patsy's, even if Max has seen fit to cancel our bet." At Candie's audible gasp, he went on cheerily, "Ah, I see I have struck a chord of response. Not feeling

97

quite so smug and safe now, are we?" As he spoke he kept moving, not stopping until he had effectively backed her into a corner of the room. "You asked why I am here tonight. I think we are both about to discover the answer."

Candie pressed herself against the wall, her blonde head slowly moving back and forth in wordless denial of the inevitable. She should scream for help. She should faint away at his feet. She should give him a swift kick in the shins.

So why couldn't she open her mouth? Why did she feel more awake, more vitally alive than ever before? Why, if there was any physical contact to be made between the two of them, did she want it to be with her lips, her arms, her tinglingly anticipating body?

He took her mouth first, capturing her lips beneath his fleetingly before tracing small, nibbling kisses down the length of her slender neck to her shoulder. Finding her hands with his own, he raised her arms to twine around his neck, and when she did not resist, he trailed his fingers down her arms and began a devastating exploration of her soft upper body.

"Ah, my torment," he breathed against her ear as he maneuvered the two of them over to lie close together on the waiting bed, "I have longed for this since the moment we first met. Come, my sweet Candie, let me love you."

Candie was beyond protest, beyond denial. Her guardian angel, usually so alert to danger, was dismissed without a qualm as the woman in Candie gloried in an entire world of newly discovered sensations. If she were to be damned for anything, she would gladly be damned for this.

Tony was an experienced lover, and it took him next to no time at all to dispense with the robe that hindered his wandering hands. Now he could feel her softness as it beckoned beneath only a thin covering of silk. He would love all of her, taste and touch her from head to toe. But first he had to have another sample of her sweet lips. Nibbling at the corners of her mouth, he used his tongue to coax her lips apart before deepening the kiss.

And then, suddenly, he drew back. Candie, slow to realize that the man who had so recently been draped half across her willing form was now arching away from her, his body rigid with shock, moaned at her abandonment and, her eyes still shut tight in bliss, reached up to coax him back into her embrace. Her hands met rock-hard muscle, taut, unyielding muscle, and she opened her eyes to gaze at him through slightly out of focus sherry eyes. "Tony?" she questioned shakily.

His eyes raked her silk-encased body one more time before glaring at her accusingly. "Damn you, Candice Murphy!" he spit out between clenched teeth. "What trick are you planning now?"

She didn't understand. What was he talking about? Hadn't he been doing the seducing? She watched in bewilderment as he practically threw himself off the bed and put half the distance of the room between them.

"Cover yourself!" he hissed, averting his eyes. "What if m'sister were to come in and see you like that? Or is that what this is all about? All that talk about never marrying was all a hum, wasn't it? You're out to catch yourself a husband, aren't you? Well let me tell you, madam, you've set your cap at the wrong man!"

Now Candie was angry. *Very* angry! "What the devil are you babbling about? You barge into my life, set my entire formerly pleasant existence all topsy-turvy, make me abandon every vow I've ever made—not to mention depriving me of my hope of Heaven without allowing me the luxury of enjoying the sin—and then you turn around and accuse me of having designs on *you?* You're a few bricks shy of a load, do you know that?"

"And you, madam, are the most crafty female since Eve," Tony snapped. "You didn't think I could tell, did you? You thought you had me so overcome with passion I wouldn't notice, didn't you?"

"My stars, the man's gone stark, staring mad," Candie said to the room at large. "That's what it is. The man's become unstrung."

"Oh really?" he sneered. "I may have been a little unhinged earlier, but not so much as to overlook the fact that you, my little schemer, are a *virgin!*"

Candie was nonplussed for a moment. Of course she was a virgin. But how did he know? And what difference did it make? "Guilty as charged, my lord," she admitted at last, just as she thought he was about to explode once more. "I'm a virgin. Since when is that a crime?"

Coniston ran his hand through his hair, a habit Candie realized to be an unconscious gesture of frustration. "Give me some credit, for God's sake," he said curtly. "I may be many things, but I am not a despoiler of virgins." He slammed a fist into his palm. "Damn that wily Max! He knew it all along."

At last Candie understood. Tony had been more than willing to bed her when he thought her to be a woman of the world, but now that he had discovered her innocence he didn't know what to do with either her or his own desires. Unbelievably, she felt very much like smiling. "What's to do now, Coniston?" she quipped, settling herself on the edge of the bed.

Lost for a moment in a brown study, Tony's head jerked up at her mocking words. If looks could kill, Max would have soon been throwing a fine Irish wake for his only niece, but Candie felt no fear. "What I do now, you maddening chit, is to go somewhere private and get roaringly, messily drunk."

Candie watched as he headed for the window. Just as he put a leg up on the sill she asked softly, "And what then, Tony? How do we deal together in the future?"

Tony turned to look at her over his shoulder. "We don't," he answered tersely before disappearing out of sight.

Chapter Eight

TONY WAS true to his word.

Four days had passed since he'd uttered his vow in Candie's bedchamber, and no one, not Patsy (whose only comment was that Tony must be hot on the trail of yet another dashing matron), or Hugh Kinsey (who stared at Candice very intently but said little), or Will Merritt (who hadn't even realized that his friend had done a flit) could shed even a glimmer of light on his possible whereabouts.

Max, being Max, had *not* been true to his word.

He had remained ensconced in his suite at the Pulteney for the full three days he'd alloted for the scheme before returning to Half Moon Street, having departed the hotel disguised as himself, his booty (and some fine wines discovered during a nocturnal tour through the Pulteney cellars) dutifully lugged to the street by a willing lackey. All that remained behind of the Maharajah of Budge-Budge were a small mound of soiled ceremonial robes and a large unpaid bill of fare.

After appearing in Portman Square to offer his thanks to Lady Montague for "sheltering my dear lamb whilst I was away" and present the lady with a fine Sèvres vase as a small token of his appreciation (seeing as how his pawn-broker had offered only half its worth), he agreed that Candie should remain where she was for a space, as his schedule was rather hectic.

Upon his asking for and receiving Lady Montague's permission for some moments of privacy with his niece, their hostess departed to have a word with Cook, who had performed some distressingly distasteful act upon last evening's turbot.

The door to the small salon had barely closed behind Patsy's departing form when Candie, standing in the middle of the room with her arms crossed at her waist, asked baldly, "How much?"

Max didn't dissemble but calmly reached into his pocket to pull out a roll of notes as thick around as his fist. "I left decent vails for the servants, of course, and the advertisement set me back a trifle, but the rest is here, lassie, all right and tight. Now if you could just see your way clear to gifting me with a pound or two for walking-around money? It's the barber I'll be visiting, and there's a hole starting in my left boot sole, and no mistake."

Candie nodded, barely listening to her uncle's recital of pressing needs. She counted out over a thousand pounds of pure profit—surely enough to keep them warm and dry for some months to come. Unless Maximilien had another sudden urge to visit his favorite gambling hell, that is. "Here's two hundred, *Uncail,* " she said, holding out a small pile of notes and depositing the rest in the bodice of her morning gown. "That should keep you in shoe leather for a little while."

"It's a hard heart you have, lass, and no mistake. Is it casting me off you're about to be, now that you're swimming in Lady M's deep gravy boat?"

"Oh, close your potato trap, *Uncail,* and give your

tongue a holiday," Candie admonished cheekily before gathering Max into her arms and giving him a smacking kiss on the cheek. "I missed you, you know, conniving r͏ ͏l that you are."

Max was pleased to see that his niece hadn't allowed her friendship with Lady Montague to turn her head. But what about Lord Coniston, he couldn't help but wonder. Disengaging himself from Candie's fond embrace, he held her at arm's length and looked into her eyes searchingly. "And what about Betancourt, puss? Is he why you're here? And is it pursuing the man or hiding from him that you're doing?"

"Ha!" she expostulated. "As if hiding behind his own sister's skirts could keep me safe from such as him." Her brown eyes took on a dreamy look as she remembered Tony's nocturnal visit to her boudoir, then clouded as she remembered his parting words. "His lordship was a bit put out by my slight breaching of his family walls, but he took himself off several days ago to God knows where, so I imagine he can't be too upset. Not that I care a fig where he is, mind you," She shrugged her shoulders eloquently. "Ah, well, while the cat is out the mouse will dance, right, Max?"

"So it's cat and mouse you two are playing, is it? He came to see me at the Pulteney, you know, ranting and raving at how I was going to land you in jail, or worse. Wasn't nice of you to set him on me, not that I couldn't handle him."

Candie smiled. "I heard. You gave him that 'please God' rubbish, didn't you? Seeing as how it took you three days to show your cheery face in Portman Square, I imagine God's pleasure was not required. I'm sorry for setting the man on you, but I could tell he wasn't about to stop hounding me until I told him what I knew. I had no fear that you couldn't fob him off some way." Giving Max another kiss, she proceeded to sit herself down on the settee and pat the space next to her. "Come here and let me tell you about a visitor Patsy had while you were away."

"Ivy Dillingham?" her uncle suggested, wrinkling his pudgy nose. "Tony mentioned her to me. Can't say as I knew of his connection with the old harpy. How is she? A year older and a year worse, I wager."

"Why not stay to dinner and judge for yourself? Mr. Merritt and Mr. Kinsey are already invited. I do believe Patsy wishes to use them as a cushion against Miss Dillingham."

Maximilien considered the idea a moment and decided an evening spent with Ivy Dillingham might be entertaining. But he said, "Perhaps I can amuse the woman."

"You plan to pluck the same fat hen twice?" Candie asked, seeing the twinkle in her uncle's eyes.

Max shook his head. "No need, lass. We're sitting solid for the moment. I just thought I'd flatter the creature a bit—keep her viper tongue off you and her ladyship for a space."

Candie gave a little shiver. "I won't ask how you know Patsy's frightened to death of the woman, but I'll agree to anything that will keep Miss Dillingham diverted, at least during dinner. Honestly, the woman's enough to put even a trencherman like you off your feed. Besides, I think she could be dangerous."

"Covets her brother's wife's goods, y'mean?"

"Exactly." Candie nodded in agreement. "I could see her toting up the worth of every scrap of furniture in the place when she was here the other day. Not that she would do murder or anything like that, but she bears Lady Montague little love. I wish Patsy could be rid of her. If only she'd open her eyes to Mr. Kinsey. He'd protect her."

"Candice Maureen Elizabeth Murphy," Max chided, clucking his tongue. "Since when did you need a third party to do your dirty work for you? This soft living has dulled your wits and mayhap your courage as well. Ah well, if you're too soft to do the thing yourself I guess I might be persuaded to take a hand in things."

Sitting up very straight, Candie retorted just as her uncle had known she would. "The devil you will, you devious old conniver. If I decide Ivy Dillingham must go, I'll handle the way of her going m'self, with no help from you at all. The apple doesn't fall that far from the tree, you know, and I've learned a trick or two of my own over the years."

"How will Betancourt react if you go sticking your nose into what he clearly believes to be family business?"

A slow smile lit Candie's face and she sank back against the settee. "I don't know, Max. Actually, I think he's beginning to get used to it."

"Oh, Mr. Murphy, you shouldn't say such things!"

"Of course I should, ma'am," Max soothed silkily, "for it is naught but the truth. You really do have the most incredible eyebrows I have ever seen. They are like soaring birds, lifting my spirits with them as they glide through the heavens. I tell you, Miss Dillingham, it fair unmans me to be in the presence of such a woman as yourself."

"*Ohhh*, Mr. Murphy!"

"Come, my dear, and we'll walk a bit in the garden. It's so unseasonably warm tonight. On my way here, as a matter of fact, I do believe I felt a bit of a fairy breeze. Perhaps we'll come upon a band of fairies traveling from one of their forts to another. We must say a short prayer, and no mistake, as there's no knowing if the good people are bent on doing good or evil."

"A prayer, Mr. Murphy?" Ivy Dillingham repeated, picking up her shawl and heading for the doorway to the garden. "Are these fairies anything like leprechauns? Perhaps we'll find their pot of gold."

Leave it to the old bat to bring the conversation back to money. If the creature were only ten years younger, five stone lighter, and had a new face, Max mused, I might just enjoy this little stroll. Aloud, he explained, "Ah, my dear lady, the leprechaun is ever more crafty than the fairy. You see them in the shade of the evening or by moonlight such as this, hiding under a bush mending a shoe. If you're very, very quiet, you can sneak up on one and—"

Max's voice faded as the two passed through the door to the garden, leaving a bemused audience behind. All through dinner Max had handled Miss Dillingham through a combination of blatant flattery and unbelievable tall tales, until Patsy had risen to her feet to signal an end to the meal before her sister-in-law could so forget herself as to proposition Murphy at table. Now, sitting beside Candice on the settee, she turned to her new friend to exclaim, "Did you ever before see the like? 'Incredible eyebrows' the man says. I should say so! She shaves them off, Candie, did you know that? Those soaring birds are nothing but glued-on mouse fur! Has your uncle gone senile?"

Looking at Patsy, her pretty face flushed with indignation, and then over toward Will, who was silently mouthing the words *mouse fur?* and pulling a face, and lastly at Hugh, whose twinkling eyes were the only indication she had that he had noticed the undercurrents that had been threading through the dinner conversation, Candie at last gave in to her mirth. "Max is blarneying Miss Dillingham, Patsy. He means no real harm, but with Max, if he's not fishing he's mending his nets. Always trys to gather allies to him, Uncle Maximilien does."

"Does Max often find himself in need of allies, Miss Murphy?" Hugh asked, easing himself away from his stance near the fireplace and seating himself in a chair nearer to the women.

"A person can never have too many friends, Mr. Kinsey," Candie replied slowly, fixing her sherry gaze on the man. "Besides, Max means no harm. He's only 'codding' her. Not that my uncle is above a good joke if the spirit hits him."

"It's a shame Tony couldn't be here with us tonight," Hugh told the group. "Off at his shooting box at Grantham

I believe, though I can't imagine what he'd want up there all alone. Now there's a fellow who would appreciate your uncle's performance here tonight. Will, you remember that to-do Tony stirred up while we were at Cambridge. I'll never forget the look on that professor's face when Tony owned up to what he had done."

"It was marvelous all right," Will agreed, a wide smile lighting his face. "I only wish I had thought of it, but I've never been the sort that could dream up such a clever stunt. None too bright, you know," he acknowledged, inclining his head toward the ladies.

While Patsy went about assuring Will that he was indeed very clever, Candice asked Hugh to tell her about Tony's Cambridge prank.

The young Marquess, Hugh cheerfully informed them, was ever one to enjoy knocking the stuffing out of the pompous, posturing sort of know-it-alls that considered themselves to be superior to the rest of mankind. Indeed, weren't his so-called scribblings all satires of the great? While at Cambridge, Mr. Kinsey went on, Tony was cast in the way of a certain professor of antiquities who thought himself the world's best critic of ancient sculpture. "You know the sort," he said, looking toward the ladies. "His was absolutely the final word on the subject."

"Like Ivy Dillingham?" Candie asked, tongue in cheek.

"Like peas in a pod," Will concurred, trying to ignore Patsy's halfhearted objection.

"Anyway," Hugh went on, "one fine day while we were all digging at some Roman site or another as part of our class, one of the fellows unearthed a marble sculpture of an early Roman goddess."

"Can't say as how it should have caused all the ruckus it did," Will interjected, shaking his head. "Missing its nose, it was, and half a leg. Dirty too, of course, being stuck underground like that all those years."

"If I may continue?" Mr. Kinsey said coolly, giving his friend a meaningful look. "Will is correct, however. The goddess was a little the worse for wear. But we dragged her back to the professor's laboratory anyway, where that good man examined the statue at length and proclaimed it to be a prime example of early Roman sculpture. Called in the press and everything, the man did."

"Must have been more than a score of them hanging about when Tony showed up," Will interrupted, wiping tears of mirth from his eyes.

"Indeed," the primary teller of the tale went on. "It was a full house all right. Well, there was the professor, puffing out his chest and pontificating about his great find when in walks Tony, a marble nose in his hand, half a marble leg tucked under his arm, and the female the sculptor had used as a model, large as life, draped on his other elbow. Tony had commissioned the statue, you see, then buried it where he knew the class was digging. Depressed the professor's expectations of glory no end, I tell you."

Now Will took over the conversation. "It was a lark, all right, but it doesn't hold a patch to the time dear Tony borrowed his mama's genuine elephant-foot table and made a long trail of suspicious-looking tracks all along the banks of the Serpentine. The trail led *to* the lake, you understand, but none led out again. Half the town was convinced someone's runaway pachyderm had come to grief. In *three feet* of water! There was even a committee of concerned ladies who petitioned the government to drag the lake. Tony volunteered to have the beast stuffed and put on display at Astley's if anyone could raise it."

"I didn't know that," Lady Montague chortled delightedly. "And to think, Mama was on the committee! It's no little wonder he never confessed to that particular prank."

Candie was highly diverted by these tales of Tony's antics, making her feel closer to him, in spirit if not in person. Hugh's earlier conversation had supplied her with Coniston's probable whereabouts, but it seemed he was seeking solitude not only from her but from his closest friends as well. Why she felt responsible for Tony's retreat from society she did not know—after all, it wasn't she who was pursuing him—but it afforded her not so much as a smidgen of satisfaction to know that he was running away from his attraction to her.

If Coniston were less noble, less of a gentleman, he would have stayed and made good his threat to bed her. But his discovery of her virginity had thrown him into confusion, his honor vying with his lust. Remember that, Candie, she told herself sternly, remember that Tony desires only your body, not your affection. Now, she informed herself dolefully, you understand the definition of limbo, for that is where you reside. Neither fallen woman nor marriageable miss, you are destined to inhabit a sphere where you are considered an untouchable.

"Yoohoo, I say, Miss Murphy," Will called, interrupting Candie's unhappy thoughts. "I asked if there weren't a tale or two about your uncle you'd wish to impart to us. I'll bet you have a whole storehouse of pranks the wily Max has played, seeing as how his blarneying, as you called it, worked such a miracle on old prune-face."

As her latest bout of introspection had only served to make her feel even more sorry for herself, she was more than happy to steer the conversation away from Tony, the man responsible for her alarmingly frequent bouts of self-pity, and toward Max, the one man who could read her with a single, piercing look. Before her uncle reappeared in the room, she had better put a bright face on things or else prepare herself for a stinging lecture on facing "reality" the next time the two of them were alone.

Candie sat front in her seat and looked around her at the three expectantly waiting listeners. "Let me think," she began, tapping her index finger against her chin. "Max's little pranks are more self-serving than the Marquess's, seeing as how my uncle can't see the sport in the thing unless a sum of money or other prize is in the offing."

Will bobbed his head in agreement. "Tony warned me never to bet against Mr. Murphy, telling me that the man was a—pardon my words but remember they are really Tony's, not mine—'odds-stacking, silver-tongued conniver of the first water.'"

"How coincidental that you should mention betting, Mr. Merritt," Candie slid in smoothly just as Hugh's judiciously applied toe brought Will to the realization that not only had he opened his mouth to put his foot in it, but he had stuffed Coniston in there as well. "The episode that first comes to mind took place after a very boring dinner party during which our host delivered the most flagrantly self-serving monologue extolling his own virtues, talents, and lucrative business dealings that it seemed to me the man was just *begging* to be taken down a peg or two.

"Well, Max, who had been sorely trying my patience the whole evening long by agreeing with every word the man said and even adding to the man's inflated image of himself by blarneying the man in a way that would make his performance tonight with Miss Dillingham seem like he had been insulting the lady, finally took umbrage with one of our host's statements.

"The man had been assuring us that he was known far and wide as the premier billiards player in the land. 'Not so,' challenged Maximilien P. Murphy, 'as I am the best billiards player, not only in this land, but in all of Europe.'

"Our host challenged Max to a game, of course, and we all adjourned to the billiards room to witness their epic combat. 'I'm the better player,' announces Max, bowing to his host magnanimously, 'so I'll play *left-handed.*'"

"Oh, I say, jolly sporting of him, giving himself a handicap," commented an impressed Mr. Merritt.

"Yes, indeed," Candie replied, lowering her head to hide her smile. "Max won, of course, gaining for himself not only the heartfelt thanks of the rest of the guests, who had waited a long time to see their pompous host bested, but a fat purse of gold from the loser as well.

"Our host remembered his manners well enough that, as we were about to descend the stairs to our carriage, he belatedly complimented my uncle's play, then remarked, 'I would like very much to see you play right-handed if you can do so well using your left.'"

"Here comes the catch," Hugh whispered close by Patsy's ear.

Candie heard and smiled. "'Oh, I don't do nearly as well,'" she quoted Max as having informed his victim. "'You see, my good sir, I *am* left-handed.'"

The small party was still laughing as Max and Ivy Dillingham reentered the room, the former to be heard waxing poetic over the lady's pleasing speaking voice (that in reality assaulted the ear like a fingernail dragged across a slate board) and the latter still lapping it all up like a sow at the trough.

"Do you play?" Max asked his companion as they neared the pianoforte, and then retreated to a chair between Hugh and his niece as Miss Dillingham prepared to regale her audience with a piece she knew from memory.

"Ah, I don't believe I know that one," Max whispered to Hugh in an aside. "But we Irish have a saying—'It's the tune the old cow died of.' Good thing we're in the city, else many a milkmaid would find herself out of a job come morning, and no mistake."

"Mr. Murphy," Hugh whispered back, "I don't know just what it is you have up your sleeve, but I'm in your debt for diverting Miss Dillingham this evening. I do believe Lady Montague is beginning to crumble under the strain of her sister-in-law's vile tongue and depressingly more frequent appearances in Portman Square."

Max shrugged off the compliment and looked Hugh square in the eye. "Why don't you do something about it then, laddie? Her ladyship is no match for that grasping harridan. She needs a strong man to send Miss Dillingham about her business before the woman decides to take up permanent residence."

Hugh bristled momentarily at Max's censure, but was

alarmed enough to ask, "Do you really think she'd actually try to move in?"

Throwing a beaming smile and a small wave to the woman still brutally persecuting a fine musical instrument, Max answered out of the corner of his mouth, "That's a body that would come for a wedding and stay for the christening. When she wasn't busy trying to drag me into every dark corner in the garden she was telling me how costly it was to keep her house open in town so as to keep an eye on poor Harry's widow, watching to see she does nothing to shame his memory or some such rot. She's been gnawing at Lady M's door for close on to two years now, I hear, and I believe she's about to sink her jaws into the poor dear herself. Sure of herself is our Miss Dillingham, so sure that she just may have overplayed her hand. Never show your teeth till you're ready to bite, I always say, but then women ain't as subtle as men. There's still time to head her off, if you're a man of action."

Hugh Kinsey chewed on his knuckle as he looked from Miss Dillingham to Lady Montague and then back again. Never before had he seen such an uneven match. Where was Tony when he was needed, the man thought angrily, then berated himself for looking to others when it was *his* Patsy whose happiness was at stake.

"I wonder if Will and I could—" he began, thinking out loud.

"Mr. Merritt is only fit to mind mice at a crossroads," Max cut in, sensing the direction Hugh's mind was taking. "Not that he isn't a fine gentleman, much like many of his fellow fribbles, but the Dillingham is considerably above his weight. You'd be better served to enlist my niece in your cause. At least she's got a brain under her hair. Will Merritt has naught but a 'To Let' sign under his."

Her party piece completed, Miss Dillingham accepted the thin applause with a condescending inclination of her head and, as there was no vacant chair near Max, sat herself down next to Patsy and began listing her complaints concerning their recent meal.

"We sent a fortune in shrimps back to the kitchen, my dear," she pointed out, waving a pudgy finger in Patsy's face. "You'll not see them again either, for I saw the footman eyeing them up as he carried the platter away. And five removes! Really, such extravagance is not seemly. Harry would not stand for such waste. You'll run through your inheritance before another year is out if you keep up this mad pace."

"Speaking of waste,"Candie cut in, addressing Patsy, who seemed to be shrinking in front of her eyes, "I don't believe I've told you about Max's shocking interpretation of picnicking. While I had envisioned a leisurely meal spread out on a blanket beneath a shady tree, Uncle had ordered the coachman he'd hired to merely drive through the countryside while we ate our meal inside the coach. When we were done, he lowered the window and, ignoring my protests, tossed everything—silver, glasses, tablecloth, uneaten foodstuffs, utensils—out onto the roadway. Can you imagine that!"

"Only way to picnic without a mess," Max proclaimed, winking broadly at Lady Montague.

Miss Dillingham could not bring herself to censure her new suitor (and the only suitor to show up for more than thirty years, and that one was only after her dowry), instead smiling weakly before returning to her attack on her sister-in-law.

"Your inept management of the Montague kitchen does not begin and end with tonight's shrimp, my dear. I have been monitoring your extravagances for quite some time, which is why I have availed myself more frequently of your dutiful invitations to dine with my only living relative. I fear for you," Miss Dillingham declared in patently false tones. "How could you, untrained in matters of economy, continue to exist once you've frittered away my, er, my *brother's* fortune?"

"I could give her a lesson or two," Candie piped up, anxious to put an end to the woman's harangue before Patsy wilted away before her eyes. "In times of low financial tide I've always found the lowly potato to be my greatest ally. A tasty, nutritious food, it can be served so many ways, like champ, which is potatoes mixed with chopped scallions, or pandy, the name we give to potatoes dipped in butter, and even praties, a filling dish of raw grated potatoes, flour, salt, and a bit of milk mixed together into cakes and fried on a hot stove."

Ivy Dillingham cast Candie a fulminating look. "I find your descriptions extremely unappetizing. You Irish must eat more than potatoes. Do you never serve fish or meat? How uncivilized."

"Only eat fish on Fridays, don't you know," Max piped up, following his niece's lead and employing a broad brogue, "and that's because I have to. But we Irish eat meat—when we can get it. There's a wealth of Irish beef that sees only an English platter, more's the pity. Candie, tell Miss Dillingham about our potatoes and dip."

Silently blessing Max for falling in with her intention of shocking Miss Dillingham's sensibilities to the point where she'd opt for a temporary retreat from Portman Square rather than spend any more time with such vulgar commonfolk as the Murphys, Candie promptly explained that when times were good a family would dip their potatoes in a common bowl of meat gravy before eating them. "And then, when times were bad, we'd have to settle for another dish, potatoes and point. That's when we'd all skewer our potatoes on our forks, point our utensils at a strip of bacon placed in the center of the table, and then pop the plain spud into our mouths."

Miss Dillingham, her scented handkerchief pressed to her mouth, mumbled her excuses and bade Patsy call for her carriage. As she was sweeping out of the room she paused, turning to cast a last regretful look at Max, who had seemed such a promising suitor until his common Irish heritage had surfaced and she had been forced to recall the duty owed her ancestral name. He would be crushed, she was certain, remembering his barely hidden passion in the garden as he likened her ear to a miniature seashell, but she was not about to make a cake out of herself like Harry by letting her heart rule her head.

"I will call on you again next week as usual, Cleopatra," she warned before quitting the room. "With your parents gadding about creation without giving you a thought, never mind the poor example set by your brother, the time has come when I can no longer sit idly by and watch you make a shambles of your life. Harry would want you to be guided by me, you know that. And I believe it is time we consolidated our households."

Candie had to scramble in her ladyship's reticule to find the sal volatile she then waved under Patsy's nose in order to keep that poor lady from swooning dead away. "Vile, nasty woman," Candie gritted, giving the now empty doorway a withering look. "How I'd like to do that old witch a mischief!"

"Indeed?" Max queried lightly, rising in preparation of making his own departure. "And is it my blessing you'd be wanting, lass, before you do the deed?"

"Now just a minute, please," Hugh cut in, seeing his one chance to be of service to Patsy—and perhaps getting her to look at him in another light—slipping away from him. "I may have made a sad hash out of it to date, but my sole aim in life is to keep Lady Montague from any sort of unhappiness. If anyone is going to deal with Miss Dillingham it is I, Hugh Kinsey."

"Why, Hugh," Patsy breathed, lifting her melting blue gaze to her old friend's face and feeling a most delicious flutter beginning deep in her breast. "How masterful you sound."

"Really?" Will asked, looking at his friend curiously. "Funny—reminds me of the play last week at Covent Garden. Chockful of lofty declarations and feats of derring-do.

I say, Hugh, you ain't thinking you can challenge the old bat to pistols at dawn, are you?" He shook his head. "Won't do, you know. Pity, that. She's so broad even you couldn't miss her, poor shot that you are."

Hugh waited patiently until Will slowly wound himself down and had lapsed into confused silence before extending his hand to Max and thanking him once again for his help with Ivy.

"Enjoyed it, lad," Max admitted before bowing over Patsy's trembling hand. "Your servant, ma'am," he said conventionally, then added, "you've a kind, charitable heart, my lady, but a foolish one. The time has come to rid your gentle self of a burden that is not yours. In other words," he ended, broadly winking his eye, "if Harry's sister wants to take care of her family—tell her to go with her brother. That's the sort would feel right at home in a graveyard, and no mistake."

With the party now reduced to four members, all of them in a somber mood, it was some time before anyone made an attempt at polite conversation. After weakly discussing the latest scandals, the same old scandals merely being replayed with a different cast of bedroom-hopping characters, they lapsed once more into silence until Candie, her temper still urging her to take action, said aloud what they all had been thinking: "We have to get rid of that woman somehow."

"Poison?" suggested Will, momentarily removing the knob of his cane from his mouth to add his bit to the discussion.

Hugh shook his head, amazed that he had even momentarily included Will in his unformed crusade to oust Miss Dillingham. "Will, it pains me to say this, but when it comes to being a lamebrain, you bear off the palm. Poison! My God!"

"Now, Hugh," scolded Patsy, taking in Will's crushed expression. "He meant well. It's all my fault anyway. If I weren't such a cowardly peagoose I'd have sent Ivy to the rightabout myself. Harry would be the first to encourage me to cut her off. He never could stand his sister, you know. But I *am* the only family she has. Besides," she sighed, hugging her arms about her shoulders, "I'm terrified of the woman."

"What does Tony say?" Candie had to know. She couldn't understand why he hadn't helped his sister with her problem.

Patsy gave a shrug. "Tony? Oh, no one was ever more provoking. When I complain to him he says I'm making a big to-do out of nothing. 'Deny her entry,' he says as if it were that simple. What am I supposed to do? Arm the footmen and have her expelled at gunpoint? Oh," she groaned pitifully, "she's going to move in here and take over my *entire* life, I just know it!"

"And your entire fortune," Candie said under her breath. Well, not if Candice Murphy has anything to say about it, she won't! Ivy Dillingham could only move into Portman Square if she were physically in London. All she, Candie, had to do was to arrange it so that Ivy's ample body was removed from the city—not permanently, that would be too much to hope for—but at least long enough for someone to coach Hugh Kinsey in the proper approach to courting Lady Montague.

"Have you people ever heard of the ingenious prank someone who shall remain nameless played on a certain Mrs. Tottenham back in 1809 right here in London? It caused quite a stir at the time, Max told me, as I recall he was delighted by the brilliance of the joke even while he was envious that he hadn't been the one to conceive it."

"Tottenham. Tottenham," Hugh mused, tapping his fingers on a side table until his memory cleared and a decidedly wicked smile lit his normally noncommittal features. "I remember now. The woman fell afoul of old Hoo—Whoops, sorry, I almost gave it away. She fell afoul of *someone* who devised a most ingenious revenge. Poor woman retired to the country for over a year, trying to live it down. And to repair her shattered nerves, I don't doubt. Miss Murphy, *that* was a wicked, a very wicked, prank. Surely you aren't considering—"

"Aren't I?" Candie purred, tilting her head to one side and smiling sweetly. "Can you think of a better way to get Ivy Dillingham out of the way? Other than poison, I mean."

Patsy, whose memory did not extend beyond last night's dinner menu, had been hastily put in the picture by Will, who assured her over and over that it was a jolly good idea.

Patsy's tender heart fought her burning desire to have Ivy Dillingham banished, however temporarily, from her life, and, in the end, her tender heart was told to mind its own business. "It is a totally reprehensible notion you are suggesting, Candie dearest," she said with an attempt at severity before throwing her arms out wide and chortling, "Let's do it!"

"Mr. Kinsey?" Candie urged, crossing her fingers and hoping Hugh would see the coming escapade as a way to Patsy's heart. "Are you going to refuse to take part in such a madcap prank?"

Hugh looked to Will, wiggling excitedly in his chair like an overage schoolboy longing to go on a spree, and then to Candie, whose mischievous sherry eyes were daring him to join in on the fun, and lastly to Patsy, who was nervously gnawing her full bottom lip while searching his expression with her huge, innocent blue eyes.

And then Hugh Kinsey did something that forever altered Lady Montague's notion that he was no more than her good and loyal friend, mayhap a bit too stuffy and solemn for her taste at times, and certainly not a romantic figure by any stretch of the imagination.

What Hugh Kinsey did was to rise to his full height and, placing his hands on his lean hips in the best swashbuckler fashion, announce loudly, "Refuse, you say? What? And miss all the fun?"

"Thank you, Blessed Virgin," Candie murmured under her breath.

"That's the ticket!" Will shouted, clapping his hands.

"Oh, Hugh!" Patsy gushed, jumping to her feet and throwing her arms around her brave champion, who stood there, or so Candie thought privately, grinning like the village idiot.

Chapter Nine

IT HAD BEEN a long, exhausting day, the second of what the conspirators judged to be the three days of concentrated effort necessary to concluding phase one of their plan, and Candie was more than happy to enter her chamber to see the covers turned back on her bed and her nightgown arranged neatly across the pillow.

She had just opened the third button on the bodice of her simple gown when a slight noise that sounded ominously like someone clearing his throat reached her ears. Whirling about to search the darkened corners of the room, she hissed softly, "Who's there?"

"A gentleman caller," said a voice from the direction of the window, and the Marquess of Coniston, looking extremely weary, a bit disheveled, but still devilishly handsome, stepped out of the shadows to make his bow.

"I see no gentleman here," Candie retorted nastily, wanting nothing more than to throw herself into his arms and smother his dear face with kisses.

"First trick to you, madam," Tony acknowledged, lowering himself into a chair near the fireplace. "Shall we try again? You say 'Who's there?' I believe, and then I say 'A rakehell, libertine caller,' and then you say—what do you say, Miss Murphy?"

Try as she could to hold her heart firm against him, her features softened and she said sympathetically, "You look tired, my lord."

"No, I don't," he contradicted, rubbing a weary hand across his eyes. "I look exhausted. Exhausted and hung over, no thanks to you."

"Me? Well, if that isn't the outside of enough! You're just like Max whenever he falls off the water wagon. That man can go for months without a drop of whiskey—even lord over his friends with his pure-mouthed airs and sanctimonious bleating—only to fall off that same wagon with a mighty splash and embark on one of his, if short, definitely *dedicated* benders. And when he awakes with a pounding head and a mouth dry as cotton what does he do? He blames me, that's what he does. Says I drove him to it by asking him to please hang up his coat that he threw on the floor or some such lame excuse. Now you're blaming me for your dive into a bottle. Well, I won't have it, you hear me. I won't!"

Coniston winced and brought his fingertips to his temples in hopes of massaging away some of the pain. "I hear you, madam, as does half of London. Unless you want Patsy in here, I'd consider it a kindness if you'd lower your voice to a quiet shriek. There seems to be an echo living inside my head, and loud noises set it off."

Candie went to the pitcher sitting on a bureau in a corner of the room and poured Coniston a cool glass of water. "Here," she said, holding out the container grudgingly. "It's my tooth glass, but it will have to do unless you want the servants to know you're here."

Tony downed the contents greedily and returned the glass, holding her hand when she tried to move away. "I knew you couldn't just heartlessly dismiss me in my distress. I just got back to town tonight. I could have waited for morning—cleaned up this mess I am a little bit—before presenting myself, but I was afraid I'd lose my courage if I put it off."

"Pot-valiant, not courageous, Tony," Candie pointed out, letting him know she realized he had to fortify himself with liquor in order to face her. "If you needs must be half seas over in order to work up the gumption to apologize for your last midnight visit I can tell you that you have abused your liver to no good purpose. I don't want your apology. I just want you to leave me alone."

Raising his head belligerently, Tony snapped, "Oh, is that right? I assure you, madam, I fully understand your demand. I too would cherish a bit of peace. So why won't you oblige and leave *me* alone, hmmm?"

Candie jerked her hand, still holding the empty glass, out of Betancourt's grip and stepped back a pace, her mouth dropping open. "Me? What are you talking about? I haven't seen you in over a week, and when we have met it was you who sought me out, not the other way round. You're drunk, Coniston," she stated firmly, shaking her head. "Out of your senses with drink. Go home and get some sleep."

Now Tony laughed, but it was a laugh devoid of humor. "Sleep, she says. That's a fine joke. How can I sleep when you're in bed beside me, taunting me with those dancing bedroom eyes, teasing me with the sight of your unbound hair cascading over your breasts? Damn, woman, like Shakespeare wrote, you've murdered sleep for me."

"Oh, Tony—" Candie began sympathetically, reaching out to lay a hand on his shoulder.

"Don't touch me!" he warned, shaking her off. "Let me say what I've come to say and then—but no, first things first." Pushing himself out of the chair, he lowered himself to one knee and grasped her two hands between his. "Miss Murphy, I have come here tonight for the express purpose of asking you to become my affianced bride. I have admired you from the—"

"Stop it!" Candie exclaimed, vainly trying to free her hands.

"Nonsense," Coniston rebutted. "I'm only halfway through my speech."

"You're halfway to Bedlam if you think you can barge in here in the middle of the night, admittedly more than three parts drunk, and make a May Game of me with some asinine proposal of marriage you won't even remember making come morning."

"Now that's not fair, Candie," Coniston objected, rising unsteadily to his feet. "I know just what I'm saying. You're a virgin, so it's marriage or nothing. After all, you're not some brass-faced lightskirt—pity, be easier then, wouldn't it—so there's no other way."

"How very flattering," she pointed out in a cold voice. "And you figured out this scheme all by yourself, did you? Funny, it smacks of something Will Merritt would have dreamed up. Besides the fact that you have combined your proposal with an insult that is unforgivable, your speech is glaringly devoid of any reference to tender feelings or even mild affection for me. Indeed, if I could somehow find a way to gift you with my eyes and hair I dare say you'd be just as happy to dismiss the rest of me."

Tony let his gaze run the length of Candie's trim body. "Oh, I seriously doubt that, sweetings," he drawled wolfishly.

Suddenly, Candie had had enough. Snatching her hands away, she whirled and stomped halfway across the room before spinning about once more to face her tormentor. "This is all moon madness anyway. A Marquess can't wed a penniless nobody of no background. What would your parents say? Somewhere in that wine-befogged mind don't you understand that you are above my touch?"

"Am I by God? By whose standards? Society's? Conventions? Or your warped sense of insecurity? Our marriage will be no more than a nine days' wonder before some other gossip comes along to distract the tattle-mongers. And as for my esteemed parents, they'd probably give a ball in your honor, seeing as how they've been begging me for grandchildren. You do like children, don't you?" he asked, eyeing her owlishly.

"Of course I do! But that's beside the point. We are not going to be married."

"Don't you like me?" he asked, trying hard to look crestfallen and not succeeding a mite. "Even," he held up his thumb and index finger, "a little bit?"

"You know I like you," Candie said peevishly. "That's not the point."

"Then what is the point?" he asked, advancing on her with his arms spread wide. "Look, sweetings, I've never done this before, this proposing thing, and I must say I didn't think I'd make such a hash of it, but I really do want to marry you. Please"—he grinned imploringly—"have some pity on a desperate man. I haven't slept a wink in a week."

Candie was perilously close to bursting into tears. How she longed to be gathered into his arms and swept away from the real world and all its problems. But someone must remain clearheaded. It would never work, this marriage he spoke of so blithely. She was a bastard who would bring shame upon his family; a nameless nobody shunned by polite society.

If he loved her as she loved him, they could fight their detractors together. But he only desired her, and once that desire was satisfied, she would be nothing more than an embarrassing burden.

"Go home, Tony," she said at last, watching as he swayed wearily on his feet. "You'll be able to sleep now that you've talked to me, and then once your head is free of drink and fatigue we'll talk again. If you still want to," she added softly, doubting that he would be of the same mind in the sober light of morning.

"Go home," Tony parroted, running his fingers through his disheveled hair. "Talk again later." He nodded his head. "All right. But I'll be back, sweetings, see if I'm not."

Candie steered him toward the door, not believing he could negotiate the drainpipe again in his condition without coming to grief, and warned him to let himself out quietly.

"G'dnight, sweetings," he said, his kiss landing somewhere on her chin, before he tiptoed clumsily down the hallway.

"Goodbye," she answered, wiping a tear from her cheek before softly closing her bedroom door.

"How very enterprising of you to secure us this excellent vantage point, Hugh." Lady Montague praised the man sitting beside her as she surveyed the view through her dainty mother-of-pearl opera glasses.

"Best seats in the house," Will concurred, his seafaring Uncle Bartholomew's spyglass resting across his knees as he sipped from a crystal wineglass Candie had handed him.

A thick sheaf of closely written papers held in her hands, Candice Murphy sat on a chair placed in front of another smaller window that looked out over the street, her head bent over as she read from the topmost paper. "The bakers should be the first to arrive. There should be two dozen of them, if my figures are correct, all carrying five-tiered wedding cakes meant for the happy event."

"As close as Ivy Dillingham will ever get to a real wedding," Will commented. "Uh-oh, here comes the first one. Bit overdone, what? All those pink rosebuds and trailing ivy cluttering up the thing."

As the four interested observers watched from their borrowed viewing box—Hugh's second cousin's bachelor residence—the bakers began wending their way to the Dillingham town house, one by one at first, and then in a sort of iced confection procession, all to be turned away by a flustered housemaid who insisted they had the wrong address.

Next came a growing rumble of discordant sound as dozens of young boys ran before their customers calling "Sweep! Make way, make way! Sweep!" as they cleared the way for the two score of clergymen enroute to minister to the distressed soul who had summoned them for spiritual guidance. The narrow street was well on its way to being clogged with black-clad bodies toting Bibles when ten draymen pulling wagons loaded with beer barrels began vying with each other to stop at Miss Dillingham's tee-totalling door.

By now the housemaid had ceased closing the door on each applicant for admission and merely stood in the open doorway, wringing her hands in her apron and begging for everyone to go away.

As the first hour melted into the second the flood of humanity rose to high tide as dozens upon dozens of tailors, upholsterers, bootmakers, hatters balancing towering piles of merchandise, and grocers pushing heavily laden vegetable carts battered against the now closed and barricaded doorway, insisting they had appointments with Miss Ivy Dillingham.

And they did have appointments—all preplanned to keep a continuous stream of humanity pouring into the congested street, tying up traffic and creating a general nuisance sure to make Miss Ivy Dillingham very unpopular with her neighbors as well as the laughingstock of the entire city.

"Oh, this makes it all worthwhile," Patsy gushed, clearly delighted with the scene beneath her window. "When we were writing out all those invitations and summons to service I thought it might all come to nothing, but it has succeeded beyond my wildest expectations."

"The originator of the prank may have written out four thousand invitations, but I think the two thousand we sent were sufficient," Candie said, once again checking her list. "As it's almost noon, I do believe the traveling coaches should be arriving soon, sent for to carry 'the newlyweds' off on their honeymoon."

As if on cue, the traveling chariots and four appeared, and within moments the street had erupted into bedlam, the chariots all impeding one another as they struggled to reach the same goal, the horses rearing and plunging as their drivers cursed and sawed on the reins.

The four schemers enjoyed a delicious picnic lunch as lawyers eager to write wills, doctors carrying instruments for the amputation of limbs, artists anxious for commissions, fishmongers bearing cod and lobsters, butchers lugging legs of mutton, filthy coal heavers, and undertakers delivering coffins in which to display the deceased became the targets of the increasingly hysterical Ivy Dillingham's demands that they all go away and leave her alone.

"The coffins were a nice touch," Hugh Kinsey told Candie, who acknowledged his compliment by raising her wineglass to him.

There were, as the day wore on, some omissions of invitations that had contributed greatly to the official inquiry the original prank had set off. The Lord Mayor had not been invited to tea with a visiting dignitary, the Governor of the Bank of England and the Chairman of the East India Company had not been advised that they could learn of ongoing fraud in their companies if they answered their summons, and the Duke of Gloucester was not told that a dying woman, once an attendant of his royal highness's mother, would make a confidential communication of the greatest importance if he were to present himself at Miss Dillingham's, but then the four conspirators were not anxious to have their part in the chaos of the day discovered.

By four of the clock, the last of the two thousand had come and gone, leaving the street looking as if a war had been waged on the cobblestones between the flagways, and it seemed only fitting that the last summons of the day brought a man drawing a fully loaded hay wagon, commissioned to spread straw on the street outside Miss

Dillingham's in preparation for an imminent "blessed event."

Ivy Dillingham's ancient traveling coach, with hastily stuffed bandboxes tied to its top and its curtains drawn on its occupant, tracked silently over the straw as that harassed lady opted to rusticate at the small country estate dear Harry had left her rather than stay and face the repercussions (and the bills for services rendered) the days' events were sure to bring.

"A toast, my friends," Hugh said, filling his companions' wineglasses. As they all raised their glasses he intoned solemnly, "To a successful rout. May she not stop running till she reaches John O'Groat's!"

"Here, here!" his companions seconded and, downing their drinks in one gulp, they all turned and hurled their glasses into the fireplace.

"Through sulking, are you?" Max remarked upon first encountering Betancourt on Bond Street. "M'niece said you were back in town, but she was close as an oyster as to how she knew. Still trying to turn her toes off the straight and narrow? It won't work, you know. My Candie's one in a million. Not like you English."

Tony was in no mood for Max's taunts. After sleeping the clock round and rising with a head that still housed a few discordantly clanging bells, he had allowed a further twenty-four hours to pass before daring to venture out into the sunlight once more.

A belated but nonetheless distressing recollection of his abominable behavior in front of Candie on his first night back in London had so far kept him from calling on the ladies in Portman Square, for even though he was still resolved to wed Candice, he was deuced embarrassed over his poor handling of his proposal.

The last, the very last thing the Marquess needed was to be forced to endure Murphy's pointed jibes and veiled innuendos as to Candie's possible rejection of his suit.

"Now what's the matter with Englishmen?" Tony at last asked Max, concentrating on what he decided would be the lesser of two evils.

"Greedy devils, all of them," Max explained. "Would toss their own grandmothers out into the cold if there were a penny to be made in the process. That's why you're missing the mark with my Candie. Money and baubles mean less than nothing to her. You won't win her by dangling diamonds under her nose. Now take your English females—"

"I have," Tony cut in facetiously, a lopsided grin lighting his previously grim features, "in regular doses since my middle teens."

"Ah, 'tis a right fine scoundrel you are," Max laughed appreciatively. "But avarice is not limited only to the fair damsels of your land, but is evenly distributed throughout the whole of England, from chimneysweep to Duchess."

"I do believe I should make exception to that remark, perhaps even call you out, but I imagine you have some way of proving your point. Am I right, Max, do I scent a wager in the air?"

"Not a wager, lad," Max contradicted, "merely a learning experience, aimed at showing you your countrymen as Candie has been made to see them. Candie, like all the Irish, is the *real* aristocrat. To my niece food is considered nourishment, clothing naught but warmth, and shelter anything with four walls and a roof. She disdains fripperies and niceties as nothing more than gilding on the lily. Nothing puffed up or pompous about the Irish, my lord. It is you English who put so much store on appearances and the accumulation of wealth. Beneath our rags beat the heart of the true aristocrat; strip an Englisher to the buff and you have naught but naked greed."

They walked on together a few paces while Tony sorted all this out in his head. Then, thinking he had just the right rebuttal, he said, "But Candie says she will not wed me because I am above her. My title and wealth seem to impress *her.* "

Max shook his head. "Candie don't give a snap for your title or your gold, you daft man," he contradicted positively. "But *you* do! It's you she's thinking of when she turns down your proposal. She did turn you down, didn't she?"

"As if you didn't know."

"I didn't," Murphy admitted, hating to show Coniston how his control over his niece had slipped a notch so that she no longer confided in him. "I knew she liked you, any fool could see that she had allowed her head to be turned by your pretty face, but I didn't know things had come to this point. So tell me, what are you going to do about it? Put your tail between your legs and run away?"

"Isn't that what you'd like me to do?" Tony asked, looking at the man intently. "Lord knows I have you to thank for warning her off."

"And what else could I be doing but my duty, being her only relative still above ground? Yet, to tell you the truth, lad, I've been doin' a bit of pondering on the subject and I do believe I've found myself softening a bit. You'd be good to my Candie, I'm thinking, and I'd sleep easier at night if I thought her future secure, don't you know."

Tony stopped in his tracks, so surprised was he over this last statement of Murphy's. "And is it sickening for something you are?" he asked in a broad affected brogue. "Besides being a dedicated rake, I'm an Englishman into the bargain. I find it hard to believe what you're saying, not that I'm not happy to hear it."

Max's ears turned a bright red. "There's English and then there's English, though it pains me dear to say it. You're one of the good ones. Having met more than a few of the bad ones, I've learned to tell the difference. So has my niece, although she has another reason of her own for shying away from you."

"I know she's not ashamed of being Irish," Tony reasoned aloud, "so it has to come back to this business of rank and wealth. Damn and blast, Max, if her being poor and having to live by her wits don't bother me, why should it bother her?"

Max looked at his young friend a moment, trying to gauge whether or not to confide in him, then shook his head and changed the subject. "Ah, here's a fine-looking jewelry store. Just what I need to prove my point about your countrymen. Care to join me, lad?" he asked as he turned to enter the prestigious establishment.

Knowing that no amount of questioning about Candie would accomplish anything once the Irishman chose to end his confidences, Coniston only shrugged and followed after the man, willing to allow himself a bit of amusement.

Once inside, Max poked about a bit, eyeing various pieces of jewelry that lay in glass-topped cases before purchasing a rather inexpensive bauble that he requested be placed in a box bearing the establishment's name. Then he motioned Tony over into a corner and, opening the box, lifted out the bauble and replaced it with a quantity of brightly colored various sized pieces of glass he poured from a pouch he had extracted from his pocket. Replacing the lid of the box, he gave Tony a broad wink. "Now we'll have a bit of fun," he said, bowing the Marquess in front of him through the doorway.

Max took no more than three steps onto the flagway before he pretended to stumble, the jeweler's box tumbling from his hands and spilling open upon the ground. To the untrained eye, it appeared that a considerable fortune in emeralds, diamonds, and rubies was bouncing and rolling about in the dust at their feet, and the resultant chaos was all that Murphy had known it would be.

Tony, pushed rudely against the front of the jewelry store by the sudden crush of people bent on scooping up some of the jewels for themselves, could only gape open-mouthed at the sight unfolding before his eyes. Sweeps jockeyed with painted dandies, ladies of quality risked their finery to scrabble on their knees beside painted women of the evening, and bankers, sportsmen, and valets scuffled like urchins fighting over a toy. When he spied out his recent mistress, Lady Bledsoe, clutching a particularly large green stone to her bosom and screeching, "Mine, mine I tell you!"—his look of incredulity faded, to be replaced by a smile of unholy glee, and he clapped Max on the back in congratulation of a point well expressed.

"Max, to quote Syrus, no Irishman you understand, but a good man for all that, 'Society in shipwreck is a comfort to us all.' Why it should so amuse me to see my fellow man brought so low I cannot tell you, but I must agree you have proven your point to a fare-thee-well."

The older man, slipping a hand around the Marquess's elbow, merely smiled his agreement before urging his friend to join him in breaking a bottle or two at a nearby inn. "It's a great thirst I seem to have worked up this morning, don't you know. But then, who needs an excuse to drink with a friend, hmmm?"

As he paid down his blunt for two bottles of the inn's finest, it never even occurred to Tony that any motive save pure friendship lay behind Max's cherubic, smiling face.

Chapter Ten

LIVING IN Portman Square, surrounded by luxury and being treated as if she were a real lady, was beginning to appeal to Candice more than she would have cared to admit. It was almost as if she had been born to such luxury, such elevated status. She felt comfortable with Lady Montague and the several members of the *ton* Patsy had introduced her to, and as the days had passed into weeks, the idea of going back out "on the road" with Max lost more and more of its allure.

There were times, even as her finer self tried to deny it, that she immensely regretted turning down Betancourt's drunken proposal, if only so that she could continue to live in the style to which his sister had accustomed her. But no, her finer self always reminded her, that wouldn't be fair. Besides, it wasn't really the luxury of soft living that so seduced her; it was the absence of worry over where she would next lay her head, when she would next be able to fill her belly, what she would do when Max's good luck finally ran out, that lent such a rosy glow to her current lot.

Walking idly about the morning room, absentmindedly touching her fingers to an art object here, trailing her hand over the curved back of a satin settee there, Candie tried hard to convince herself that all she would miss once she and her uncle finally put London behind them was the house in Portman Square. Oh, how hard she tried.

What is he doing to me? her tortured mind screamed loudly inside her head. Why is he torturing me so? What have I done to deserve this terrible punishment?

The object of Candie's silent questions was, obviously, one Mark Antony Betancourt, who had appeared in this same morning room every day for the past week to bow over her hand, spend precisely one half hour conversing civilly on the weather and the latest on-dits of society, and then take himself off again. Never did he bring up the subject of his late-night visit to her bedchamber. Not by the flickering of an eyelash did he acknowledge that they had unresolved business between them, that he was still waiting for an answer to his proposal, that he cared any more for her than he did the flowers that he brought her daily.

"I bid you good morning, ma'am," said a voice from the doorway, so startling Candie that she nearly upended a vase as she whirled to face the person whose actions, so very unexceptionable in any other gentleman but so out of character for him, had over the course of the last week nearly reduced her to nervous spasms.

But not this morning, she vowed silently as she stiffened her spirit. Not if I have anything to say in the matter. Gifting Coniston with her brightest smile, she cooed sweetly, "Come to play propriety again, my lord? Tell me, are you in training for taking holy orders? You have become so circumspect in your actions of late that I do believe, if Patsy is serious about giving a ball next month, you will not be able to find it in your prudish heart to dance on more than one foot. Come," she said, spreading her right arm wide and motioning toward the solitary straight-backed chair he had occupied on all his other visits, "sit yourself down, my lord, and let us wax poetic over the rain that seems to be showing no signs of stopping. That is what you came by to discuss, isn't it?"

Tony allowed one finely chiseled eyebrow to rise as he took in Candie's high color and belligerent stance. So she'd had enough, had she? Max had advised him to court her as he would any gently reared female, he told her, the idea being that Tony should win her heart with gentle wooing, but it now looked like the time had come for more than polite phrases and a few moments spent gently fondling her hand. "Madam," he ended, striving for some measure of dignity, "I have spent the past week striving my utmost to be deserving of your regard."

"Have you now?" Candie asked, seating herself on the settee and eyeing him curiously. "Then I imagine it would sadden you to know that you have fallen far short of the mark. The only thing I have found you to be this past week is a crushing bore. What I don't understand is why you would bother to go to such extremes. Have you committed some terrible faux pas for which you hope to atone by way of turning yourself into a tiresome society gentleman?" She knew of what transgression she spoke, but if he *had* forgotten his drunken proposal it wasn't she who was about to mention it!

Candie saw Tony stiffen at her allusion to his poor behavior the night he had made such a muddle out of asking her to marry him and took secret delight in his discomfiture. "So that rankled, did it, my lord? How very gratifying to see that you are not suffering from some dread loss of memory." She was being mean-spirited she knew, but she considered herself to be the injured party in this affair and getting a little of her own back seemed to be only fitting in the circumstances. Perhaps Betancourt would take Max to task for the failure of this latest strategy, scoring for herself yet another point, as Max, who had hauled himself off in a fit of sullens after berating her for neglecting to inform him of his lordship's proposal, had no right to interfere with her life in this matter—no right at all!

There was a pregnant silence while Coniston refigured his strategy. That he should drop his pose of gentlemanly suitor seemed obvious, a point which he would discuss with Max at length when next he met up with the once again elusive Irishman, but now he was left with deciding which of the several options now open to him would prove most beneficial to his suit. Looking at Candie, beautiful in her belligerence, he found himself feeling proud of her for not allowing this charade of civility to continue when they had already come so close to the ultimate passion. Dare he say what was in his heart without branding himself a hardened seducer? Should he give in to the nearly overwhelming impulse to crush her in his embrace, or would that damn him forever as a man who craved only her delectable body?

At last he found the silence to be even more discommoding than Candie's incisive questions, and broke into speech, giving voice to the first thing that popped into his head. "I admit to taking your uncle's advice, sweetings, but only because such a device as he suggested is not new to me. You remember that I told you a hobby of mine is rewriting other's literary works? Well, at the time Max suggested this bit of tame courting, reworking our *relationship* seemed to be a capital idea! Now, alas, it appears such a strategy has served only to blow the last of my hopes to bits."

"Perhaps you should keep to fiddling with plays like John Grey's *Love in a Tub* and refrain from diddling with your personal relationships for fear of tumbling into a real bubblebath?" Candie suggested, tongue in cheek.

"Ah, Candie, my sweet," he said, smiling in relief as he made to gather her into his arms (believing he had at last landed on the right stratagem), "what a great deal of time we have wasted."

Neatly sidestepping his encircling arms, Candie retorted, "Don't you dare try to put some of the blame for your latest descent into idiocy on my doorstep, my lord. And *don't*, for pity's sake, compound your stupidity by thinking I shall now drop into your arms like a ripe plum and let bygones be bygones. You are not *that* irresistible, you know."

"*Idiocy? Stupidity?*" Tony fairly shouted back at her. "One of these days, madam, you will go a step too far! What must I do to make you understand that I am serious in asking you to marry me? Better yet, why on earth do I *want* to marry such a shrew? Lord, Shakespeare had a tame kitten in Kate if only he knew it."

"Perhaps rewriting that little tale should become your next project," Candie replied scathingly. "As for me, I would rather retire to the country to raise dogs than spend another moment in the same room with such a conceited womanizer as yourself. Good day, sirrah!" Candie turned, indicating her intent to quit the room.

Tony snaked out an arm as she swept by him and roughly hauled her about by the elbow. "Oh no you don't, missy. If I am to be condemned as a man sunk to irreclaimable depths of depravity, I might as well live up to my sordid reputation." So saying, he pulled Candie unceremoniously into his arms and captured her lips in a brutal kiss. She fought him for a moment (mainly due to the discomfort his grinding mouth was inflicting, although he wasn't to know that), before he could feel her body melting beneath his questing hands. As her resistance ebbed he allowed some tenderness into his kiss, and that tenderness set off a mutual spark of passion that soon had them clinging to each other like shipwrecked sailors hugging a bit of flotsam to keep from drowning.

When it became impossible to continue the kiss for lack of breath, Tony raised his head a fraction of an inch and crooned unintelligently, "Do you see now how very compatible we are, you irresistible Irishwoman? Come now, admit I'm right and be done with it."

There are times when a wise man resorts to action, times when words aren't enough. This was definitely one of those times. But Coniston, being a man and therefore prone not to know when to leave well enough alone, had chosen to open his mouth and destroy what could have been a major victory.

Candie's once more stiffened stance gave him his first clue as to his error. Her firm little palm, making stinging contact with his left cheek, succeeded in removing any lingering doubt as to his glaring error in judgment. The slamming of the morning room door behind Candie's departing back was like the coffin lid coming down on all his fondest hopes and dreams.

And the whole of it couldn't have happened to a more deserving fellow!

"A-a-a-choo! Good God, that's all it needed! You! Stop cringing and come here!"

The servant who had just set down yet another bottle at Lord Coniston's elbow shuffled indecisively a moment or two before taking a few quavering steps forward. "Who sir? *Me,* sir?" the man asked in a frightened voice. "Whatever did I do, sir?"

Sitting as he was in the dirty end of the coffee room at Boodle's at the unfashionable hour of two in the afternoon, and being quite the only other person in the vicinity, Coniston took exception to the servant's implied suggestion that he could possibly have meant anyone else. "Yes, my good man, I mean you," he gritted, rising to his feet. "As to what you have done, why, I think that I should be obvious. Your periwig reeks of dust. Why else do you think I sneezed?"

"Your snuff, sir?" the servant was foolish enough to suggest, motioning toward the open box in Coniston's hand.

"Damn and blast! Am I to be contradicted on everything I say today?" Tony asked the room at large. He had been drinking steadily since arriving at the club, seeking to ease his bruised sensibilities (while holding a cool bottle to his still smarting cheek), and, besides trying to drown his sorrows, he was in dire need of expressing himself in some physical manner.

"Give that to me," he commanded now, pointing to the offending hairpiece.

"My—my periwig, sir?" the servant questioned, beginning to shake.

"I'd just as soon have your liver," Tony offered, an evil grin lighting his intimidating expression. "The choice is yours."

"But—but—" the servant stuttered, hesitating.

Tony's slender hold on his temper slipped entirely from his grasp, and with a muttered oath he snaked out his hand and yanked the offending hairpiece from the man's head. Looking about for some handy place to stow the thing, he spied out a spittoon and, with a violence that served to totally unhinge his hapless victim, hurled the periwig into the brass pot.

It wasn't many minutes later that the starch-backed majordomo appeared at Coniston's elbow to say, "That periwig, sir, was the property of this establishment. I'm afraid I was forced to put it on your bill."

Tony looked up at the man, his dark eyes twinkling. "Very well, my good man. Never let it be said I refuse to pay for my little pleasures."

"Yes, your lordship. But there remains the problem of James Oglesby."

"Who or what is a James Oglesby?"

"The servant you accosted, my lord," the majordomo informed him. "He's highly overset. I can't see how I can get him to work at all for the remainder of the day."

The Marquess shrugged his broad shoulders. "Gad, that is a disaster, isn't it? Very well. Put him on my bill as well—and add a guinea or two for his injured sensibilities. Now, if we're quite finished, I'm trying to get drunk here, man, and you're disturbing my concentration."

The majordomo bowed himself from the table, satisfied that he had both protected Boodle's good name and warned the young Marquess away from any further disturbance of the staff.

"Put him on my bill," Tony chuckled, wondering just how the majordomo would phrase the charges. "One purloined periwig—£2.6. One overset Oglesby—£3.2. It's a good job I didn't decide to take exception to *him* as well. I can't imagine how the fellow would settle on a charge for one manhandled majordomo."

"Talking to yourself, Tony? I can't believe that's a good sign." Hugh Kinsey pulled out a chair and sat himself down beside his friend. "Patsy told me you'd been to see Miss Murphy again today and left in a bit of a huff. I've been searching you out up and down the street for over an hour."

"And now you've found me. Congratulations," Coniston drawled sarcastically, wondering if he was ever to get any peace. "I'll put in a good word for you in Bow Street. I imagine they always have room for another good Runner. Can't say as how a red vest would become you, though."

Hugh pursed his lips and gave a silent whistle. "A little out of sorts, are we? Perhaps my business should wait till another time."

Tony's interest was piqued. "What business? Are you in some sort of trouble, Hugh?"

Smiling sheepishly, Hugh leaned back against his chair and quipped, "That, my dear friend, would depend on one's particular feelings regarding matrimony. I'm here to ask your permission to pay my address to your sister. She's not adverse to me, you know, and we've gotten on quite famously ever since working shoulder to shoulder on that little prank we organized to oust Miss Dillingham."

"Shoulder to shoulder, eh, Hugh?" Tony teased. "No

closer than that? I've always known Patsy to be most demonstrative in her affections."

Hugh blushed scarlet to the roots of his hair. "If I had known you were going to be crude I would have sought out your father, wherever he might be at the moment. As she's a widow, asking formal permission for Patsy's hand is only a formality, but I thought it fitting to consult you in the absence of the duke."

"In that case, Hugh, I'll be more than happy to give you my blessings, just as my father would do—right after he fell on your neck in gratitude. Lord, he was so worried he'd never marry off my adorable, widget sister that he gave her to Harry Dillingham. Widow or not, I wouldn't be surprised if the old man sprang for quite a wedding present, so grateful will he be." When Tony saw that Hugh's usually placid face was taking on the look of an approaching thunderstorm, he added, "Besides, I couldn't think of another man more suited to making Patsy the happiest woman on earth."

"You really think so?" Hugh's expression suddenly became as bright as the sun breaking through after the rain. "Fool that I am, for a man of my advanced years, I do love her. It's strange, don't you think, this love business?"

Tony stared at his friend owlishly. "How am I to know?"

Hugh shrugged, trying to be subtle as he, like many a moonstruck man before him, tried to ensure that all his single friends should be made as happy as he. "Will says you're in love, seeing as how you're camping on your sister's doorstep while Candie is in residence." Now it was Tony's turn to resemble a thundercloud. "Ah well," Hugh hastened to add, "you know Will. Jumping to conclusions as usual. Only exercise he gets, I dare say."

Taking another long drink from his glass, Tony subsided in his chair and stared into the middle distance. Hugh watched his friend anxiously. This was not the Tony he knew. Oh yes, he had seen him upset before, in moments of frustration or boredom. But never before had he seen

Tony evince self-doubt, which was how Hugh chose to interpret Coniston's strange expression.

"Well," Hugh challenged, deciding to take the bull by the horns, "is Will off the mark as usual, or did he strike a nerve? Are you just hanging round Candie's skirts because you're afraid she and her uncle are out to fleece Patsy? If so, I believe I already told you I don't believe a word of such nonsense. Candie's a good sort, I can tell, although I'll admit she's a rare handful, no thanks to her uncle's upbringing of her. But Patsy and I both think she's a grand girl. Perfect for you, actually."

"You'd think so, wouldn't you?" Tony retorted acidly, stung into absolute honesty. "Then how do you explain the fact that the chit has refused to marry me? *Twice!*"

Hugh's estimation of Candice Murphy, already complimentary, went up another notch. He had known from the beginning that Tony was more than casually attracted to the girl, but to have brought the great Mister Overnite to his knees was no mean feat. "Does she know that you love her?" he asked after a small silence.

Tony banged his glass down on the table with unnecessary force. "What the blue blazes does that have to do with it? I wouldn't have asked her if I didn't mean it."

"Mean what?" Hugh persisted. "That you want her in your bed, as you so arrogantly announced to me that first night, or that you love her with all your heart and can't imagine life without her?"

Now Tony sneered. "Coming on a bit strong, aren't you, Hugh? Next you'll be penning novels for the Minerva Press."

Hugh just smiled and shook his head. Poor Tony, alternating between balancing on his high ropes and bawling like a sick calf. For as mad a rake as Tony to be so laid by the heels was a gratifying sight to see. "You love her," he said now with soft conviction.

Running a hand through his hair, Tony blustered, "All right, all right. Have your pound of flesh, Hugh, you deserve it after all my teasing about Patsy. Yes, damn it all, I love her!"

"Does she know?"

"Of course she knows!" Tony fairly bellowed, sending yet another servant scampering for cover.

"You've told her?" Hugh urged reasonably.

"Of course I've—*good God!*" Tony leaned toward his friend, grabbing Hugh's arm and giving it a shake. "Wouldn't she have already figured it out? I mean, Candie's very bright. Do you really think she doesn't know?"

Extracting his arm and making a point of smoothing his crumpled sleeve, Hugh drawled, "As I believe you have just found it out for yourself, how could she? She's bright, Tony, but she ain't a mind reader. Here now! Where are you going?"

Tony had risen so abruptly that his chair went crashing to the floor. "Where do you think?" he called back over his shoulder as he fairly trotted toward the door. "Oh yes," he added, halting for a moment. "Put your drinks on my bill. You might as well be there—everyone else is!"

"I love you."

Candie, who had been curled up in a huge chair in the corner of the library pretending to read a book, looked up at the sound of Tony's voice. Slowly shaking her head, half in disbelief of what she had just heard, and half in amazement that he was somehow standing in Patsy's library at all after their argument earlier, she whispered, "What—what did you say?"

"I said I love you," he repeated calmly, striding toward her, one hand outstretched. "Hugh said you might want to know."

"That—that was very considerate of him," Candie responded, her heart beginning to beat quite wildly in her breast.

Drawing Candie to her feet, Coniston smiled and

amended fairly, "Actually , it was Will who first noticed it. But that's not important. Hugh says you were to know, so that you might understand why I want to marry you. Honestly, Candie, I thought you knew." Candie's hands slipped up to cup his chin and he felt himself drowning in the deep-brown pools that were her eyes.

"I knew," she confessed breathlessly. "Or at least I thought—hoped—you did. But I didn't think you knew."

Tony, who had been in the process of drawing Candie more firmly into his arms, checked his movement and became quite still. "But if you knew that I loved you why did you refuse to marry me? Or don't you love me?"

"I love you, Tony. I have, for a very long time. I just can't marry you."

He didn't understand, not even a little bit.

"Blister it, Candie, you're not making any sense. And don't hand me any more of that claptrap about you being beneath me. Oh yes," he continued before she could say more than a few words, "I wasn't so drunk that I don't remember you spouting all that drivel that night in your chamber. I love you, damn it," he argued in a very unloverlike fashion, "and anyone who dared to take exception to our marriage would have to deal with me!"

"I'm more than simply poor or underbred, Tony," Candie supplied tonelessly when he had calmed sufficiently to release her arms and reposition himself in front of the window, where he stood glaring at her. "I'm a bastard."

There. It was out. Now he would understand. The Gunning sisters may have been poor when they married their titled husbands, but they weren't bastards. She couldn't bring unknown, possibly tainted blood into the Betancourt family. She loved Tony too much to do that.

"That's it?" Tony asked coldly from his battle station in front of the window, the late afternoon sun that had finally appeared pouring through the panes to make him look even more the handsome devil than he was. "My God, girl, so what? So you're a Fitz-Murphy. I could name you a half dozen respected English families who had their starts as bastards."

"Not from their female side, Tony," Candie pointed out. "There's a great difference in being the male by-blow of some prince and being the careless result of a nameless scamp and some gullible Irish girl of no background."

"But you're one of the Donegal Murphys," Tony pointed out, trying a stab at levity. "According to Max, you're descended from Irish Kings. Who gives a tinker's curse who your father was?"

Tears threatened to overtake her as she tried to make him see sense. "Max does, for one. He knows who my father was, but he's always refused to tell me. He must have been an awful man. Loving you as I do, I could never inflict his bad blood on your children." And now the tears did begin to fall. "Can't you see, Tony, ours is an impossible situation." Whirling away from his accusing eyes, she begged brokenly, "Please. Go now. When Max returns we'll both be leaving London anyway and you'll soon forget me."

His hands grasped her at the shoulders and he turned her around so that he could look into her eyes. "I'll go, love, but only to find Max and make him tell me your father's name. Your fine Irish imagination has turned the fellow into the worst of horned demons, and no demon could have fathered so sweet a girl as you. Max will tell us the truth, if only to put all your bogeymen to rest, and then there will be nothing to keep us apart." He lifted her chin with his fingertips and smiled down into her face. "Unless you really don't love me?"

"Oh, Tony," Candie whispered, flinging her arms around his neck and drawing him down to her, "I love you so very much!"

Their kiss was charged with all the passion two desperate people were capable of, and it was a thoroughly shaken Candice Murphy who watched Tony stride purposefully toward the door, a man with a mission. He would find Maximilien P. Murphy and drag the truth out of him, if need be. By this time tomorrow he and Candie would be betrothed, and nothing and nobody would stand in their way!

Tony was confident, sure of his ability to bring Candie around to his way of thinking. Loving him as she did, loving each other as they did, Coniston had no reason to doubt that there would be a speedy resolution to all their troubles.

But then, Tony had never heard of one Mr. Malcolm P. MacAdam, Esquire, and his plans for an opal mine (of all things) in far-off Scotland.

Chapter Eleven

TONY'S CONFIDENCE, which had been so high upon leaving Portman Square, began to flag a bit when he had sought out Max at all his usual haunts and come up empty. The rooms on Half Moon Street were dark and deserted-looking, and no one could remember seeing the Irishman at the Cocoa Tree or a half dozen other taverns for several days. Candie had already told Tony that Max had gone off on one of his sulks after berating her for not confiding in him as she had always done before Coniston entered her life, and she had admitted to being afraid Max could have succumbed to two of his greatest weaknesses—drinking and gambling.

After a full night and half a day spent in fruitless searching, Tony repaired to his town house for a change of clothes before heading back out onto the streets. It pained him that he had nothing to report to Candie, and he swore a silent oath that the sun would not go down on this day until he had ferreted out her delinquent uncle and pried loose anything the man knew about Candie's parentage.

He was just about to set out once more when Will Merritt came in unannounced and plopped himself down on a chair. "Came to tell you I'm not such a loose screw as you and Hugh think, old sport. Almost got myself all rolled up in some nasty scheme Geoffrey Billings told me about, but I was too smart! Knew there was something havey-cavey about the thing. Trickery, that's what it was. Base villainy. But I was too awake to fall for such nonsense. Opal mines in Scotland! Ha! That'd be the day!"

Tony, who had been about to toss his friend out and be on his way himself, stopped dead in his tracks at Will's last words. "Would you mind running that by me again, old sport?"

"Certainly," Will said, agreeable to repeating what he thought was a stunning display of his own intelligence. "Geoff showed me an advertisement in the *Times* last week about an expedition to Scotland to dig for opals. As if anyone would believe there were opals in such a godforsaken place. I mean, after all—"

"Will, would you please have the goodness to come to the point," Tony interrupted, images of Budge-Budge beginning to dance in his head.

Will rummaged in his pocket and brought out a scrap of newspaper. "Here. Read it for yourself. Geoff thought it would be whacking great fun, but I told him—"

Tony had made a grab for the paper and made quick work of reading the advertisement. The notice announced the formation of an expedition to an undisclosed location in Scotland where, so stated the notice, reliable evidence pointing to the existence of vast deposits of opal-bearing rock had recently been unearthed. The stones were there for the picking—if one but knew where to look; which is why the exact location could be divulged solely to sincere investors and then only once the expedition was on its way north.

"God give me patience!" Tony spat, waving the paper in Will's face. "And you mean to say you *believed* this claptrap?"

"I never said that. I said Geoff and his friends believed it. Though I must say Mr. MacAdam was most convincing," Will added, suddenly looking a bit sheepish. "Did you read it all?"

Tony hadn't, but proceeded to do so after pouring himself a liberal two fingers of port. A deposit of one hundred pounds ("One hundred pounds!" he repeated aloud) was to be used for mining supplies, travel expenses, and living accommodations while at the mine as well as serving to reserve the enterprising young gentleman's place in the expedition, slated to set off in exactly one week from the date of the advertisement from The White Horse in Fetter Lane.

Bank drafts, Tony read with a small sneer appearing on his face, were discouraged, as the use of currency would expedite supply procurement, and Mr. Malcolm P. MacAdam, Esquire, agent for the prestigious Peerless Engineering Company, would be at The King's Arms in Bishopgate for this one day only to answer questions and interview candidates for investment.

Crushing the advertisement into a ball and sending it sailing toward the fireplace, Tony turned to face his friend. "Start at the beginning, Will, if you please, and tell me exactly what happened between the time Geoff read you that notice and the moment you stepped inside my door today to gloat over what I am sure is your friend's misfortune. Leave nothing out."

Will looked at Coniston and said, rather testily, "Well, o'course I will, isn't that what I came here for in the first place? Honestly, Tony, although you never were an easy fellow to read, since you met Miss Murphy you've become nigh impossible to figure out. One minute hot, one minute cold, one minute—"

"Will! You've run out of minutes, just as I am running out of patience. Now start talking!"

"The least you could do is offer a fellow a drink," Will ended weakly.

Once holding a glass filled nearly to the brim (so, Tony reasoned, the story wouldn't be interrupted while the fool asked for a refill), Will told his story, beginning it, much to Coniston's gratification, at the point where he and Geoff had entered The King's Arms and met Mr. MacAdam.

"Geoff signed up straight away," he clucked reprovingly, "but I could sense something havey-cavey about the bugger—though he did have the most fantastic bright red mustache—and held back. Nothing much to talk about happened between then and yesterday, the day the fellows were all to meet up with MacAdam at The White Horse."

"Let me guess," Tony broke in, sniffing. "MacAdam never showed up, right?"

"Who's telling this tale, Betancourt, you or me?" Will asked, upset at being upstaged before he could make his own dramatic announcement. "Anyway, there they were, twenty-four disgruntled opal barons, cluttering up the departure yard at The White Horse all the day long, waiting for the man.

"After a time most of them went away, moaning and groaning, while Geoff and a few others decided to go back to The King's Arms and ask if anyone there knew the MacAdam's whereabouts. That's when they fell into a little piece of luck. One of the barmaids had found a letter or something the man had forgotten and saved it."

Tony's heart sank a little at this piece of news. Strange, he hadn't thought Max could be so clumsy. "Did this letter give them any clues?"

"That it did," Will reported, cocking his head as he looked at Tony, who didn't seem to be enjoying the tale as much as he should. "There was an address on the letter and the fellows took a Runner from Bow Street with them to see if they could find out anything about the man who had taken their blunt. And would you believe it? The man was just coming out of this place on Half Moon Street, calm as you please, as they stepped from their carriage."

Ah, Max, I do believe the luck of the Irish just took it full in the eye, Tony thought, wincing. "And then what, Will? Did he give them their money back?"

Will chuckled. "No, Geoff was too late for that. I guess the man lost it all gambling or wenching or something. They had to settle for having the bloke hauled off to the guardhouse. Hey! Where d'you think you're going? Don't you want to hear how I roasted Geoff for being so deuced gullible? Taken in like a real Johnny Raw, he was. Hey, Tony! Come back here!"

Already halfway out the door, Tony called back over his shoulder, "Be a good fellow and go to m'sister's. Tell Miss Murphy her uncle and I will be dining with them tonight. Move it man, Candie must be worried."

Will nodded his head absently in assent but did not rush to do his friend's bidding, but rather sat a few moments more, trying to convince himself that his friend hadn't completely lost his mind. "It's women, that's what it is," he decided at last. "Get yourself tied up with a woman and the first thing you know your wits are all addled. Shame," he mused, shaking his head sorrowfully, "Tony was a good man. Hate to see him taking such a bad turn."

It was a woebegone, worse for wear Maximilien P. Murphy who looked up at his visitor as the cell door scraped open and the jailer, a dirty, toothless creature, announced, "One o'the quality ta see ya. Step sharply now!"

"Ah, boyo, 'tis you," Max said, relief evident in his

voice. "And here I was just sitting here thinking as to how I could get word to you."

"'Ere now," the guard warned, "that's no way ta talk to gentry coves. Watch yer mouth, 'ear, else it'll go bad fer ya."

Murphy watched the guard depart and then turned to Tony. "What an ugly puss that fellow has," he began conversationally. "And has a smell of garlic about him strong enough to hang your hat on, don't you know." Then, dismissing the guard from his mind, he waved Tony to a seat and asked, "Now, what is it I could do for you, for you've the look of a man with a mission."

Tony eyed the rickety chair skeptically before gingerly testing it with his weight. "I've been looking for you, Max, but it seems you've been playing bo-peep with me. I'd not be here yet if it weren't for Will Merritt, who told me of your new address—not that he knows he did, you understand."

Max nodded his head. "That one! There's a slate or two off that boy's roof, don't you know. What a devil of a time I had talking him out of investing in my opal scheme. I guess he told you all about that. Ended up settling for only twenty-three shares, seeing as how I had to tell the boy I was all sold out. Wanted *two* subscriptions, mind you. If ever there was a fella wanting to be taken to the fair, it's that one. So, I guess you know I've gone and done it this time?"

"I didn't think you were here on holiday," Tony said, tongue in cheek as his eyes scanned the filthy room. "As you're still wearing that horse tail on your upper lip—Will thought very highly of your mustache, by the by—I assume you haven't given them your real name."

"What d'you take me for, a raw greenhorn? O'course I didn't. Can't take the chance of involving my Candie, can I? This was my scheme, more's the pity, and I'll take the fall alone." Max settled back against the wall and sighed. "Ah, lad, I feel just like my father, don't you know. He was always in the field when luck was on the road. A bit of gambling on the wrong dice, a bit of carelessness in leaving a trace of myself behind, a bit of greed in trying to run the same rig twice in one week—I was on my way to another inn to meet another group of investors, don't you know—and I had pushed my luck too far."

"In point of fact, Max, you left behind a rather large bit of carelessness—an envelope with your address on it."

Again Max nodded. "An invitation to dine in Portman Square," he clarified. "That was no great help to me, and no mistake. See, lad, what mixing in high society will bring you to? If it weren't for Candie's being in Portman Square there'd have been no need for a letter. If it weren't for you proposing to my Candie and her hiding it from me there'd have been no need for me to bury my sorrows in that gaming hell—not that I wasn't itching for a run with the ivories anyway. And if it weren't for losing all my money and needing to run a rig and get it back before Candie got wind of it and rang a mighty peal over my head, I wouldn't have been so careless. Do you know," he ended, looking meaningfully at Coniston, "I do believe that if it weren't for you, laddie, I shouldn't be here at all!"

Tony threw back his head and roared his amusement. "I knew you'd find a way to lay this whole thing at my door, you wily Irishman."

"Needs must when the Devil drives," Max quipped, his eyes twinkling merrily. "But I'm not complaining, you understand. I've had a fine run at life, boyo, and if I didn't knock it down, I staggered it! But, like my father, I'm not done yet. I'll be out of here in a few years, mark my word, and Maximilien P. Murphy will be even better than before! I'm like my father that way, pluck to the end. Why, Paddy Murphy was such a never-say-die that, even now, if you was to throw a halter in his grave he'd start up and steal a horse!"

"I believe you!" Tony swore, glad to see Murphy regaining a bit of his humor.

"Ah, lad," Max said with a wink, "believe me and who'll believe you?"

That brought Tony back to his senses. He already knew someone who would believe him—Candie, when he told her that her uncle was in the guardhouse awaiting transportation to Newgate. "This has been most enjoyable, Max, sitting here chatting while the rats forage in the corners, but we must put our heads together and think up some way to get you shed of this place. It's only a matter of time before someone starts digging into your past and comes up with Candie and Budge-Budge and heaven only knows what else."

"You don't want to know what else," Max put in, wincing a bit at the memory of Ivy Dillingham's face. "But don't worry your head about me. I'll not spill the soup about my own niece. No, the only problem I have now is settling Candie so that I can go to my fate without her on my mind. That's why I'm glad you're here. Lad, I have to ask you a favor. Would you take it upon yourself to care for my Candice until—well, just until?"

"Funny you should mention that, Max," Tony began, ready to tell the man just why he had been searching for him in the first place, but Murphy interrupted him.

"She's a good girl, my lord," Max said with unfamiliar formality, "and it's not her fault that she was handed a rapscallion like myself as guardian after her dear mother, bless her soul, passed on."

Hearing the pain of an old sadness in Murphy's voice, Tony urged quietly, "It must have been very hard for you both. Tell me about it, Max, won't you?"

"It seems so long ago, don't you know, but it also seems like yesterday," Max mused as if to himself. "It was in the fall of the year, and the whole county was overrun with English milords on the hunt for both four-legged and two-legged game, if you take my meaning. Brigette, my baby sister, became the prey of one of the hunters—a vile, oily creature who could weave lies as fast as a horse could trot. It was no time at all before he had Brigette believing he wanted to marry her and carry her off to his home in England."

Tony, his eyes narrowed in acknowledgement of the man's deviousness, drawled icily, "A name, Max. Give me a name."

"Lord Henry Blakestone," Max gritted and then went on to paint a verbal picture of the man that was unflattering, to say the least. The fair-haired, handsome Lord Blakestone, Max revealed, besides fathering bastards in any locality he chanced to visit in above the space of two hours, was a mean drunk, an even meaner landlord to the unfortunate tenants on his estate in Sussex, and was, in total, a truly soulless creature with all the charm of an adder and the ethics of a Covent Garden pimp. "But my Brigette was blind to all but his smooth words and his beauty. Candie may have gotten his looks but, the saints be praised, it's her mother's sweet nature she carries inside."

As he leaned forward, his elbows on his knees, Tony listened as Max told him how Brigette had been seduced by Blakestone, and how Max's logical arguments—backed up by a cocked blunderbuss aimed precisely between his lordship's heavy-lidded blue eyes—had resulted in a hasty wedding before his lordship deserted his bride and returned to Sussex and, very shortly thereafter, to his very own cozy chamber in the Blakestone Mausoleum.

"Then Candie is not illegitimate?" Coniston questioned, interrupting Max as he happily relived the moment he had stuck the business end of the blunderbuss in Blakestone's nose.

Max looked at Tony oddly. "No. Of course not. Whatever put that idea into your head? As if I, Maximilien P. Murphy, would let such a terrible thing happen."

"Candie put that idea into my head, Max. She believes

she's a bastard, and according to her, she got that idea from you."

Max ran a finger around his collar and swallowed sheepishly. "Well now, looking back, I can see where she might have gotten that idea. But it couldn't be helped, not once Brigette died and Candie and I were alone. Blakestone had a mother, a veritable viper of a woman. Compared to her, Blakestone was a bloody saint, Lord rest his soul and bless him for breaking his neck on the hunting field. I couldn't let that old witch know about Candie, don't you know, else she would have taken her just for spite. I couldn't allow that to happen to a dog, let alone my only relative."

"So you took it upon yourself to raise Candie alone. But why, once she was old enough to understand, didn't you tell her the truth?"

"Ah lad, by the time the old lady cocked up her toes Candie was nearly grown, and I saw no reason to burden her with the knowledge that her papa was a skunk of the first water. Better to have no father at all than to be saddled with a sire that made Oliver Cromwell seem like a right pleasant sort in comparison." Max looked at Tony and ended sincerely, "I meant no harm, lad, in God's truth I didn't."

Tony was silent for a few moments, thinking over what he had heard. For a moment, only a heartbeat or two in time, he questioned whether he preferred his Candie to be a bastard rather than have to number the unsavory Blakestones among her ancestors. Who was he kidding—if Candie's sire had been a one-eyed, humpbacked manure spreader, he could not love her any the less. "What of the estate in Sussex—and her inheritance?" he asked as an afterthought. "However did you find the restraint to keep from claiming the whole of it for your niece? Surely that would have been preferable to this hand-to-mouth existence you are forced to endure?"

Max smiled at Coniston's question and explained that the whole of the Blakestone estate was entailed, and in the hands of a distant cousin whose wife and seven children needed the manor house and income far more than did he and Candie. He had saved his niece from enduring a nightmare childhood in the dower house at the constant beck and call of her pernicious grandmother, and that had been enough reward.

"But enough of this talking of things past, lad," Max ended, once again coming to the point. "Will you do it? Will you take care of my Candie until I'm free? I know you want her, but I also believe it's trusting you to do right by her I can be doing."

In way of an answer, Tony rose and went to knock on the door of the cell so that the guard could let him out. "I'll take care of Candie, Max, you have no need to worry on that head, especially now that I can tell her that her ancestors are no better or worse than mine. Considering some of the blackguards whose likenesses hang in the halls of our country estate, my only fear is that she'll now consider herself above me!"

Once the door was open, Tony requested that the guard hand him the picnic hamper he had brought with him and reached a hand inside the basket. "You sit tight now, Max, not that you can do much else, can you, and I'll be off to inform your niece that you have given her over into my care. That should serve to liven up her day, don't you think? Oh yes," he added, his back already turned to leave, "and don't get too comfortable here. We can't let it be said that my soon to be wife's uncle is moldering away in some cell, can we now? Here—catch!"

And before the astonished Max could react, an apple Tony had drawn from the hamper went sailing past the Irishman's head to splatter against the stone wall.

Twisting his head about to give the man a pointed look, Tony quipped, "Slipping, Mr. Murphy? Tsk, tsk."

* * *

If Candie had been feeling a bit fretful not knowing the reason for Tony's delay in returning to Portman Square, Will Merritt's arrival and subsequent explanation had her half out of her mind with worry. For Will, not able to suppress the need to tell yet another person of his intelligence in scenting something amiss in Mr. MacAdam's offer, had regaled Candie, Hugh, and Patsy with a highly embellished version of the same story he had imparted to Tony earlier that afternoon.

"What sapskulls," Hugh was moved to say, "taken in by such a rum bite. Will, it compels the admiration, how you saw through the scoundrel's scheme. Don't you think so, ladies?"

"Indeed yes," Patsy seconded. "I believe it to be prodigiously intelligent of you, Will. Candie?" she prompted as her friend remained silent.

Candie smiled weakly. "Oh, I don't know. Seeing as how I admit to a little larceny in my own soul, I can't help but feel a little sorry for this Mr. MacAdam. Not that Will isn't to be complimented for his astuteness in seeing the fellow for what he really was. You did say you weren't taken in by him for even a moment, didn't you?" she asked, skewering Mr. Merritt with a knowing look.

"Of course I, er, um . . . the man was very smooth, I'll give him that . . . that is to say . . . *of course* he didn't take me in for even a moment . . ." Will's voice trailed off weakly as Hugh and Patsy shared a smile.

Sensing that his friend needed rescuing, Hugh cleared his throat importantly and, encircling Patsy's shoulder with his arm, made an announcement of his own. "As Tony is still detained elsewhere, and will only show up here in his own good time, I would like to share *my* happy news with you, my dear friends. Lady Montague has just this morning made me the happiest man in the world by consenting to become my bride."

"Oh, I say, Hugh, that's splendid news," Will exclaimed, crossing the room to shake his friend's hand. "Ain't in the petticoat line m'self, y'understand, but if I were I'd be glad to have Lady M to wife."

At Hugh's frown, Will quickly amended, "Not that I'll be wearing the willow now that you've snaggled her, for like I said, I'm not really—"

"Yes, Will, dear, we know," Patsy cut in, laughing. "You're not in the petticoat line. Now hush up before your tongue twists into a knot and come here and give me a kiss. After all, it isn't every day a woman is asked to become a wife."

Once Will, blushing and still stammering, had backed away from the happy couple it was Candie's turn to congratulate her friends. Years of practice at hiding her feelings, combined with the total lack of insight displayed by the two self-absorbed lovers, got her through the next few minutes as she thought about her own proposal the day before and its very different ending.

The fact that Tony had not yet returned to Portman Square, with or without her uncle, could not possibly be looked upon with other than a heavy heart. Perhaps, once he had received the information from Max that he had been seeking, Tony's ardor had at last been well and truly cooled by the sure to be terrible truth and he would refuse to have anything more to do with either of them.

But would Tony actually turn his back on them when it was so obvious that they were in need of his help? Max had a silver tongue, of that there was no doubt, but no amount of blarney could make the prison walls topple down and make him a free man. Ha, she thought in twisted amusement. As if it weren't bad enough that I'm a bastard; now I'm also the niece of a jailbird! Even the Marquess of Coniston, with all his wealth and power, couldn't fashion a silk purse of that particular sow's ear!

Just as Candie was about to lose the last remaining shred of her composure and burst into tears in front of her still celebrating friends, there came a cheerful voice from the doorway. "What ho? Is it somebody's birthday? I just passed your butler in the hallway readying a cartload of champagne and glasses."

Tony! Candie screamed silently, her eyes full of questions as she half rose from her chair and looked in his direction. He was smiling! He was happy! He was *alone!* "My . . . my uncle," she stammered, her lower lip beginning to tremble. "You did not find him then?" She couldn't have misunderstood his message. He *had* recognized Will's Mr. MacAdam for Max, hadn't he? Candie sank back in her chair, totally confused.

"Max is just where you think him, Miss Murphy," Tony informed her, this cryptic answer being supplemented by as evil a wink as she had ever seen. "He is, however, *unavoidably detained,* and has asked me to look after you until his return."

Candie would have pushed for more information but Will took that moment to steal Hugh's thunder and announce the coming nuptials, a piece of news Tony received most happily, lifting Patsy from her seat and depositing a smacking kiss on her cheek. "And they say you are a widget. Nonsense! You've picked the right man this time, puss, and no mistake. Hugh," he called, motioning the man to his side, "must I do the brotherly thing and warn you to take good care of my sister? But no, of course not. I am assured you will be the best of husbands, even when it comes to pruning away clinging Ivy, hmmm?"

"Tease all you want, friend," Hugh warned, enfolding Patsy once more in his arms, "but when love hits you amidships I warrant you'll be following us to the altar."

"If Mr. Murphy were here I'm sure he'd not take that bet," Tony offered wryly, and then proceeded to confuse his friends even more by rounding them up and ushering them none too gently toward the door. "Off with you all now and perhaps Candie and I will have some news that will have Hugh here smugly smiling for a week!"

Patsy may have been lacking in many areas, but when it came to sensing romance in the air she was as quick as the rest of her sex. "Oh, Tony, really?" she gushed, looking back over her shoulder as her brother unceremoniously shoved her from the room. "You and Candie? It's a grande passion, I knew it! Don't you dare shoo us from the room! Tony, I don't know anyone who was ever more provoking. How can you tease us so? *Tony—*"

The door closed on Patsy's tirade and Tony turned to look at Candie, who was standing in the center of the room, wringing her hands just as if she were not the most beautiful, desirable creature in nature. "Alone at last," he breathed, starting toward her.

"Could we have a double wedding, do you think?" Patsy called from the narrowly opened doorway. "All right, all right, I'm going," she blustered as Tony began to growl. "Don't put yourself in a taking. Honestly, Mark Antony, shoving me out of my own parlor. I don't remember when I—"

When Tony turned back to Candie he was holding the key to the room and, waggling his brows provocatively, he tucked it in his pocket. "As I was saying—"

Candie held out her hands as if to keep him where he was. "Don't come one step closer, please. How could you make such a May Game of me? What must Patsy and Hugh and Will be thinking right now?"

Tony smiled. "Patsy is busily planning our nuptials, I expect, while Hugh, now that the fuss is over, is probably settled down in the library reading the *Times.* As for Will, who by his own admission rarely thinks at all, I don't think we should descend into a case of the dismals over his thoughts, do you? No, I thought not. Would you then, by the by, like to know about your uncle?"

"Of course I would, you jackanapes! And stop grinning! Where is my uncle?"

"Ah, so loverlike. Well, no matter. Where do you expect him to be?"

Candie was clearly exasperated. "How should I know? Will comes in here telling me you'll be bringing Max to me shortly and then goes on to tell me about Malcolm P. Mac-Adam, who just has to be Max, and how he was caught up by the Runners." She ran a hand distractedly through her hair, a habit she seemed to have picked up from Coniston, "Can't you tell me where he is?"

Tony nodded, rather condescendingly, Candie thought. "Of course I can tell you. Max is, in point of fact, in the guardhouse. When last I saw him he was rummaging through the picnic basket I brought him. Seems I'm always bringing that man a housewarming gift."

"And you left him there? Couldn't you do anything for him?" Candie hated her feeling of helplessness, but in all their travels and travails, never before had Max run afoul of the law to this extent. She was at a loss as to how to go about engineering a jailbreak, and besides, it seemed natural for her to look to Tony for assistance.

At Candie's sad, lost look, Tony at last relented and told her what he had done. "I've already set matters in motion, love, and your uncle should be a free man by breakfast time tomorrow. Even a Marquess has limits, you know. I have, by way of a letter left with my solicitor to be delivered to Max once he is outside the guardhouse walls, suggested that Maximilien P. Murphy may have some out of the city business to attend to that cannot wait. It just seemed prudent to have him away from London for a space; at least until I can make arrangements to reimburse all the silly young gentlemen he fleeced. Pity he won't be around for our wedding, but there was nothing else for it, as I plan to have you at the altar before Patsy gets the bit between her teeth and tries to make a grand spectacle of the ceremony. Let her take care of her own, I say."

"You—you talked to Max?" Candie stammered, still finding this whole chain of events very difficult to believe.

Tony nodded his head once more. "You're no bastard,

sweetings, although I will ask you not to go inviting any of your relatives to tea, save Max, of course, when he's in town. Now, enough of this talking. Come here, you delectable creature, and this time, when you tell me you love me — please, don't shout."

It was a long, very long, satisfying time later that Candie, her head snuggled comfortably in the curve of her beloved's shoulder, mused dreamily, "Elizabeth Fitzgerald, you were a bloody fool."

Epilogue

IT WAS A small wedding, numbering only a few of Coniston's closest friends and relatives, with even his parents, those perennial travelers, not in attendance. But that did not mean that it wasn't a traditional wedding, complete with virginal white wedding gown, an altar banked with fragrant floral bouquets, and organ music accompanying the bride's march down the aisle on the arm of the fatuously smiling Hugh Kinsey while Patsy, soon to be a bride herself, wept happily into a scented lace handkerchief.

The groom, waiting nervously alongside his groomsman, Will Merritt, drew himself up proudly at the first sight of his bride, and even the few guests were heard to gasp as Candie's beauty filled the church. Her smile dazzled, as her sherry eyes sparkled, and Candice Murphy was the most beautiful woman in the world as she walked toward her beloved to begin living the happily ever after she had always dreamed about as a child sleeping on a bed of leaves beneath a hedgerow in County Donegal.

The ceremony itself passed quickly. Indeed, Patsy was to say later, the longest part of it seemed to be the unseemly passionate kiss the newlywed couple exchanged after the vows had been said.

As they walked back up the aisle, man and wife in the sight of God and man, Tony whispered in his bride's ear, "I know you must be missing Max, sweetings. I guess he felt it too soon to show his face in town. But I'll make it up to you, I swear I will. I'll settle an income on him—"

"You'll do no such thing!" Candie contradicted somewhat heatedly, making Will think once again that he was the smart one in steering clear of matrimony. "Max wouldn't take your charity. He'll do just fine by himself, just like we always did. But I do miss him. I had so wished . . . *oh!*"

Breaking from Tony's grasp, Candie raced down the rest of the aisle to a spot near the entrance.

"Twigging it," Will pronounced dolefully. "Hardly worth buying this new suit, if she's off already."

But Tony wasn't listening. He saw Candie drop to her knees beside a small wooden object lying beside the aisle and hastened to see what had attracted her attention. When he reached her she was running a hand lovingly along the carved wood side of, of all things, a cradle. Recognizing it as the one that had lately rested in a corner of the lodgings on Half Moon Street, Tony looked about for Max, who was the only one he could think of to have brought it to the church.

"I say," Will spoke from behind Coniston's shoulder, "rushing things just a tad, ain't you? I mean, we ain't even had the wedding breakfast yet."

Tony ignored his friend's latest taunt (really, having had his two best friends fall victim to cupid's dart and escaping unscathed himself had made Will more than a little cocky), and helped Candie to her feet. "What is it, sweetings?" he asked, seeing the note in her hands.

"It's a letter from Max," she told him, looking up at him with tear bright eyes. With a charming accent she read aloud, *"Aingeal cailín. Dealbh go deo ná raibh tú. Go meadaí Dia duit. Slán leat. Uncail Max."*

"That's lovely, Candie, whatever it means," Patsy, who had come to see what all the fuss was about, put in softly.

Candie grinned at her new sister and translated: "It says, 'Angel girl. May you never be poor. May God bless you. Good—'" Her voice broke a little. "'Goodbye. Uncle Max.'"

"He'll be back, sweetings," Tony crooned as Candie buried her face in his shoulder. "You know what they say about bad pennies," he joked feebly, trying hard not to admit how much he too missed the wily Irishman with the heart of purest gold. "Come now, my love, be happy. Max has given us his blessing."

Lifting her head to smile up at Tony, all her love for him in her eyes, Candie took his hand and they turned to walk out into the winter sunshine together.

From a darkened corner of the church stepped a short, pudgy, black-clad nun, her face hidden in her prayerbook. "May the sons of your sons smile up in your faces," the holy woman said in a surprisingly baritone voice before, looking about her carefully, she tipped her hand in salute and melted back into the shadows.